C000011235

A native of Bangalore, Ind
Writing and English at
upstate New York, where she is pursuing her
doctorate in English literature. Her short stories
have been published in the *Hindu*, the *Asian Age*
and the *Deccan Herald* and broadcast on BBC
Radio, All India Radio and the Commonwealth
Broadcasting Association Radio. She received the
Katha Award for Creative Fiction twice (1998 and
2002) and prizes in the Asian Age Short Story
Competition and the Commonwealth Broadcasting Association Short Story Competition, and
is a finalist in the 2002 BBC World Service Short
Story Competition.

THE HOTTEST DAY
OF THE YEAR

Brinda Charry

BLACK SWAN

THE HOTTEST DAY OF THE YEAR
A BLACK SWAN BOOK : 0 552 77121 X

First published by Penguin Books India 2001
First publication in Great Britain

PRINTING HISTORY
Black Swan edition published 2003

1 3 5 7 9 10 8 6 4 2

Set in 11/14pt Melior by
Kestrel Data, Exeter, Devon.

Black Swan Books are published by Transworld Publishers,
61–63 Uxbridge Road, London W5 5SA,
a division of The Random House Group Ltd,
in Australia by Random House Australia (Pty) Ltd,
20 Alfred Street, Milsons Point, Sydney, NSW 2061, Australia,
in New Zealand by Random House New Zealand Ltd,
18 Poland Road, Glenfield, Auckland 10, New Zealand
and in South Africa by Random House (Pty) Ltd,
Endulini, 5a Jubilee Road, Parktown 2193, South Africa.

Printed and bound in Great Britain by
Clays Ltd, St Ives plc.

For my parents, Shankar and Malathy Charry

Acknowledgements

This book wouldn't have been possible without the support of many. I am particularly indebted to my parents, as there's little I have that they haven't given; to Ravi and Premi Shankavaram, who made it so much easier to carry out this project; to Ashok and Rashmi Charry for their encouragement; to little Varun, who gives so much without knowing it; to Partha Srinivasan and old friends in Bangalore for their advice; and to J. Robert Lennon, former visiting professor at Syracuse University, who read the first few chapters and believed they were worth building on. It has been a pleasure working with David Davidar of Penguin India, who helped me begin this novel, and with Karthika V.K. and Christine Cipriani, who have been sensitive and supportive editors. Thanks also to my agent, Marianne Gunn O'Connor.

Prologue

Sudha died on a day so hot that the tar melted off the main road – the only tarred road in Thiruninravur – and stuck to people's feet in fiery black patches. Even the tough little sparrows wilted on the rooftops, and just that morning I had found a crow lying bleary-eyed with thirst beneath a tree.

It was I who pushed open Sudha's door and saw her suspended from the ceiling. It was a small room, but it suddenly seemed wide and empty. I did not go in. I stood at the door and wondered how the cotton sari she had twisted into a rope had not snapped.

It was clear, even to me, that she was dead. Though her eyes were still open, a little bit of tongue had escaped from her mouth, her legs were limp and her feet swung apart from each other, making her look like a bow-legged cloth puppet at a roadside show. Only her hands seemed alive, and I thought any minute now she might raise them to do one of the million things she had done all her life – clean her teeth, push back an escaping strand of hair, shape the rice on

9

her plate into convenient little mounds, hide the smile that might dangerously break into unseemly laughter.

But her sari and blouse were a little more crumpled than usual, and Kodai later told me that her mother had said a little blood had trickled down the insides of Sudha's thighs, leaving delicate trails of light sticky red.

Janaki must have been sleeping because she'd latched her door from the inside and didn't open it even when I knocked. So I slipped into the garden behind the house to tell my uncle Sundar. The jackfruit tree just outside the kitchen door was heavy with fruit that no one wanted to eat. One fruit lay split open on the ground, its golden entrails already beginning to rot though it wasn't really that hot in the garden, which apart from the jackfruit had four coconut trees, one mango, a gooseberry, a drumstick, a tamarind and hundreds of nameless shrubs and creepers. Tucked discreetly behind them all were the lavatory and the bathroom, their blue tin doors tilting precariously outwards. The lavatory didn't have a roof, which meant that anyone who wanted to use it during the rainy months had to carry an umbrella.

I could hear Sundar having his bath – his second bath of the day.

'Sundar Mama, Sundar Mama!' I called. My voice was shrill and lonely among the trees.

'What's the matter?' he called from inside.

Over the gurgle and wheeze of bath water going down the drain, I told him that Sudha was dead. He was silent for only an instant.

'I'll come out in a minute,' he said, and added, 'I

10

want you to wait here, Nithya. There is no need for you to go upstairs now.'

But I went back into the house, my legs light with excitement.

A beetle had found its way into the room. It buzzed noisily around my head and bumped its fat black body against the walls. Maybe it couldn't see, I thought, though the afternoon sun streamed in, making Sudha seem frail, dry and naked.

That was what worried everyone – that it was so hot. The body would begin smelling soon, they agreed, so it was better to finish things as soon as possible.

So when the police inspector came, Sundar took him upstairs swiftly. Someone was sent to bring Sudha's father from his village. He came at sunset, when she had been taken away for a post-mortem. His face was pale and bewildered, and his discoloured pancha-gacham clung to his stick-insect legs. But I noticed that he had a perfectly shaped nose – like his daughter's.

By the next afternoon, precisely one day after Sudha's death, she had been cremated. It was a simple funeral, shorn of nearly all ritual. Another police-man came to speak to Sundar, but he too went away quickly. It was a straightforward case of suicide, there was no need to worry about that. The girl who had hanged herself from the ceiling of her room with her own sari was a very distant relative of N. Sundararajan and his widowed sister, R. Janaki; her father was a priest at an unknown Srinivasa temple in Thirukullam village. Though she was never actually referred to as a *servant*, she had been doing nearly all the cooking and household chores while living with Sundar and Janaki.

A slim twenty-year-old brahmin girl, she would

11

have been married off in a couple of years once her father had scraped together enough money. They'd already managed to get her a little gold nose ring. Till yesterday it had glinted whenever she turned her face to the light, and the sun filtering through the trees in the backyard had played games of sunbeam-and-shadow with her fragile child's cheekbones, her woman's lips and the warm flesh of her brown throat.

The men who had gone with the body – Sudha's father, Sundar and a neighbour – returned by four o'clock and went to bathe before they entered the house. Janaki, a couple of other women and I sat beneath the fan in the front room. I could see that my aunt wanted the others to leave, but they waited and helped wash the house out, sweating silently over buckets of cold water that trickled out the door, down the three steps and into the street, washing away the flower petals, the grains of yellow rice, the dust of yesterday's kolam and the remnants of that unholy death.

Sudha's father left after having a tumbler of coffee. He hadn't wanted anything to eat, though we could cook now that Sudha had been cremated. He probably knew that he hadn't asked enough questions, and that he would soon have to face his wife and other children. But he couldn't have slept well the night before, and for now it looked like he was only thinking of the journey home, of how he could get some rest on the bus. Sundar sent someone with him to the bus stand and the neighbours, seeing no excitement ahead, slipped away reluctantly. Janaki and Sundar went up to their rooms, and I lay down on the freshly watered kitchen floor and felt its dampness enter the back of my head. I would go up later and explore Sudha's room once more.

And silence, as white and heavy as that summer, once more fell over the house.

Chapter One

When Amma said goodbye to me she wept a little.

'I don't even know why I'm crying,' she said, smiling uncertainly. 'It's only for a few months, isn't it?' She looked at me for reassurance, for forgiveness.

She would take the train to Madras, take another back to Bangalore and after three days fly to Kuwait with my father. Their suitcases had been packed a week ago, she'd told Janaki, trying to keep the excitement out of her voice. This was her first trip out of the country, and I knew that she was looking forward to it even though it upset her that I had to be left behind with her brother and sister. But, she had explained to me far too many times, there were problems apart from the expense of the plane ticket. She and my father were to share a stuffy little flat in Kuwait with a colleague and his wife.

'Don't worry, Akka,' Janaki said. 'I know Nithya will manage.' As always, she spoke so softly that Amma and I could barely hear her.

The train pulled away from the little length of cool

15

platform, which was almost deserted but for a woman chasing flies from slices of watermelon. She, the two mangy station dogs that lay panting under her cart, and the stationmaster, whose white uniform had been washed too often and too well with Robin Liquid Blue and was now the colour of a watery sky, watched Janaki and me leave the station. This, four hours from Madras, was Thiruninravur, the little town where Vishnu had chosen to rest during one of his long, mysterious journeys through the world of mortals. His giant purple-blue body, dipping gracefully at the waist like a woman's, would have stretched out on the red earth between the narrow meter-gauge tracks, the dusty coconut and tamarind trees, the municipal school and the deep, dark wells in the backyards of houses, with his feet resting on the blurred horizon.

Janaki sat stiff and upright in a corner of the cycle-rickshaw, her face turned away from the smooth black back of the driver. I didn't like travelling by cycle-rickshaw – it made me feel slightly ridiculous. So I examined the aerogrammes Amma had thrust into my hands at the very last minute, saying, 'One for every twenty days – don't forget.'

'So your sister has gone?' Kamala asked Janaki when we got home. Kamala lived next door to Sundar and Janaki.

Of course she knew Amma had left. I had seen her peering over the compound wall paying special attention to my mother's printed silk sari, counting and weighing her gold bangles, checking to see if she was wearing her diamond earrings. And I knew Janaki had seen Kamala watch us leave for the station. She didn't reply.

'So they'll stay in Kuwait for six months?' Kamala persisted.

'Yes, till my brother-in-law finishes his project.'

'Poor child!' She jerked her fleshy chin at me, its three stiff, black hairs like lonely little trees. 'You will miss your amma-appa, won't you?'

I stared at her. 'I may not,' I said.

Kamala looked startled. Janaki looked at me and frowned very slightly but didn't say anything.

'But you have your aunt and uncle to talk to,' Kamala said brightly. She would also ask her daughter Kodai to come and play with me every evening, she promised.

Janaki and I walked away. Kamala began plucking jasmine buds from the creeper that grew from her house but had spread impartially over both sides of the wall. I looked back to see her staring at the two of us. We entered the house and shut the door.

Now, I thought, Janaki would ask me why I had been rude to Kamala. But she didn't. She just placed her slippers tidily in the passage and went out to the pump behind the house to wash her feet. When she came back she asked if I was hungry. We'd had our lunch about three hours ago, before going to see Amma off.

'No, I'm not,' I said.

Janaki stopped at the foot of the stairs and looked at me. 'You will miss your mother?' she asked.

'I don't know.'

Janaki rarely laughed, or even smiled, and even now it didn't sound quite like Amma's laughter.

'I'm going up now. If you want anything you should tell me.' I watched her climb the stairs. She kept her

17

eyes lowered, as if she were counting the number of steps she had to climb before she reached her room.

*   *   *

Amma had told me to be careful about many things. Never to ask questions about Janaki's marriage or her husband, for instance.

'Please, Amma! As if I'm so stupid!'

'I didn't say you were stupid. But sometimes you are a bit – strange.'

'I'm not.'

But I knew I was. Like sometimes I was a witch and sometimes a shimmering Miss World in a swimsuit, with hair swept high on top of my head like a queen, and sometimes a Christian martyr smiling beatifically at the stake, watching with calm clear eyes the flames creep up my ankles and lick the tip of my white dress while the pagans stood around me wonderstruck . . . But Amma was suddenly crying because she was thinking of the sudden fever the doctors hadn't been able to diagnose and then the death of her brother-in-law, Janaki's husband, eight years ago.

'None of us could believe it, it was terrible. He was such a nice man.'

'Nice men too die, Amma. Actually they die young.' I didn't tell her that, though I had read it somewhere and thought it sounded interesting.

'And poor Janaki – she was twenty-seven years old,' Amma was saying. 'Can you imagine – a widow at twenty-seven? My mother never quite recovered from it. That was what made her so ill. She barely lived for a year after that.'

'Janaki seems to take it well,' my father had said.

18

This conversation about his wife's family, illness, death and young widows disconcerted him.

'Yes, she takes it very well.'

Amma had always been proud of her younger sister. She liked to talk about how clever Janaki had been right through school and her one year of college. 'Janaki is really very brave – she can accept things. I'm not like that, you know. Nithya has only to fall a little ill and I break down.' And she had smiled through her tears at her silly weakness.

I had stared at her thoughtfully. 'Do you think Janaki has forgotten?'

'Forgotten what?'

'Him – her husband.'

'One never forgets these things,' Amma had said sternly.

*　　*　　*

I liked Sundar's house. It was one of the sixteen houses on Govindachari Street, GC Street for short, all of which looked much like one another. There was a strip of compound in front where Sundar sometimes kept his scooter when he was at home, though he usually preferred to park it right inside the house. Behind the house was a huge unwalled garden separated from the narrow lane that ran behind the house and from the neighbours' houses by a row of hibiscus bushes. The doors and window frames were painted green, and light-yellow plaster flaked off the walls and ceilings, which dipped and bulged in un-expected places as if they were secretly pregnant. There were two rooms downstairs – a kitchen and a hall, which was always referred to as the 'front

19

room'. Both were dark even during the day because the windows and doors were kept shut. At night they were lit by the pale light of dusty sixty-watt bulbs.

Copper and steel vessels of food, smoky kitchen rags and damp gods lurked in the dusky corners of the kitchen. The front room had only a heap of footwear near the door, a radio set placed on a low wooden table and a small roll of bedding against the wall for guests. High up on the walls were a clock and some framed and plastic-garlanded pictures of my grandfather Narasimhan Iyengar, who had died when I was barely a year old; a stiff-tailed Sri Hanuman carrying the mountain of herbs; my grandmother Kanaka, who I was already beginning to forget; and the British Museum.

The rooms upstairs were far too bright, Janaki complained two days after Amma and I arrived. She tore up an old sari to make curtains for the windows of the room we were to share for the next six months. When she wasn't working downstairs, she stayed up in this room reading or stitching or just sitting on her bed. Sundar had his own room, and behind the storeroom – which held sacks of rice and tamarind, an iron trunk and an old Singer sewing machine – were two smaller rooms, one of which had been given to Sudha.

I hadn't been to the house or even seen Sundar and Janaki for five years. The only thing I remembered from my last visit was weeping furiously every morning outside the bathroom door when Amma was inside. The trees in the garden had seemed enormous then, looming threateningly behind me. Amma had come here only once more after that, by herself, and had felt guilty about not visiting more often, but I suspected she was secretly a little uneasy in the company of her younger sister, who turned quieter year after year, and her stern, hard-eyed brother, who was careful with his money and had never had much to say to his sisters anyway.

I stayed downstairs while Janaki slept. All three of them – Amma, Sundar and then Janaki – had been born upstairs and grown up here. Two other children, twins, had died an hour after birth. Their small wrinkled corpses must have been laid out here where I now sat. Amma liked to tell me the story of how the man at the burial ground, when he'd been told to get two graves ready, had dug one big one and one small. He'd thought they were for the mother and child, he'd explained when they'd arrived with the children's bodies. My grandfather had been furious.

Sundar had left a copy of a newspaper on the floor. I picked it up. The tiger in the tea advertisement looked like Sundar – lean, hard-eyed and muscled. Everyone looks like an animal if you look closely enough. Janaki was a little like a cat – not a fat-cheeked domesticated one but the other kind. Her face was fine-boned, small and very pale, with eyes that didn't give anything away. She was very slightly built, too – from behind she could be mistaken for a fifteen-year-old. But her plait was long, it went right down to her hips, and very heavy – the weight of it made her shoulders droop a little. Kamala was a buffalo, maybe a pig; her husband Vasu, whom I had seen only once, was a nice little goat. The nun who taught me algebra in the sixth standard was a goat, too. One day I would draw pictures of them all – half human, half animal – and find someone to show them to. Not Amma – she would

21

think I was making fun of her family and might decide to be offended.

I also knew that my mother was beginning to worry about Sundar's marriage. He was thirty-six years old and he should have been married years ago, she would say. Since there was no one else to do the job, she supposed that it was her responsibility to look for a girl.

'Why can't Janaki find Sundar a bride? She is the one who lives with him.'

'Janaki *Chitti*. And Sundar *Mama*,' Amma corrected me. 'Please, Nithya. You know Janaki cannot do any such thing. She is a widow.'

They had found Sundar a girl some years ago, but he had wanted the wedding to happen only after he got his appointment order from the district-government office where he now worked and after he had saved up a little. He had expected the order to come the next year, and till then would continue as an accountant for a local moneylender. That was too long to wait, the girl's parents had said. They didn't encourage such long engagements in their family.

She hadn't done anything about Sundar's wedding after that, Amma realized guiltily. Before they left I heard her tell my father that she would think very seriously about her brother's marriage when she got back from Kuwait. I wondered if things would be very different here then. What would Janaki do while Sundar's meals were being served by his bride?

It was a warm afternoon. Amma had warned me that this house had always been exceptionally hot. And it never rained very heavily in Thiruninravur – except for a few showers during Pongal. The heat

22

moved through the house like some giant primitive animal. It spread through the kitchen and front room, crawled up the stairs and hung heavily from the ceiling. I slipped my hand up my skirt and petticoat and touched my stomach, which was cold and sticky with sweat.

*   *   *

Kamala sent Kodai to see me that evening.

'It's cooler out in the garden. Why don't you two go there?' Janaki suggested. I didn't want to have anything to do with Kodai but I led the way through the kitchen. I didn't look back to see if she was following. Kodai was plump and beady-eyed like her mother. Her arms burst out of her tight half-sleeved blouse and her body, swathed in her long skirt, was a firm little tub. She looked curiously at my own knee-length skirt and striped shirt, and stopped to pick some white flowers whose name I still hadn't discovered but which I knew bloomed only at dusk.

'Janaki doesn't like flowers being picked from our garden. Especially not after sunset,' I lied. Kodai pretended not to hear me. So I went to look at the cow named Lakshmi, who had settled down for the night on the fresh hay Janaki had spread out in the shed earlier that evening.

It was Sudha's job to feed and milk Lakshmi, besides cooking, cleaning the house and buying vegetables when Sundar was too busy to stop at the market on his way back from work. But Sudha had taken a week off to go to her village because her mother had fallen ill. Sundar had given her permission, but Amma had thought it strange that she should have been allowed to go – she had been working at Sundar's house for less than a month. And it wasn't as if there was no one else to look after her mother.

The garden suddenly seemed very quiet. Kodai must have gone back into the house. I went to check. She was still where I had left her, sucking at the long juicy stamen of a flower like a greedy bee. She looked up at me but didn't say anything. Who asked her to come here anyway, I thought, to spoil my evening?

'So you too are eleven years old?' I asked reluctantly.

'No – I'm still in fifth standard,' she said, and squatted on the ground.

She doesn't want to be friends, I realized with relief. I wandered away.

'Listen!' She had come up behind me. She moved softly for someone so heavy. She was panting and had a moustache.

'What?' I asked. I wondered if I'd have to spend a lot of time with her over the next six months.

'Listen,' Kodai began, 'do you know that . . .'

'Why do you keep saying "Listen" like that? Just tell me whatever you want to.'

She was silent for a moment. 'I know many things,' she said.

'So do I, you know.' I always get first rank in class, I wanted to add. And nearly always a hundred in maths and over ninety in social studies and English. My teachers think I can catch up on classwork even though I'm missing a term from school and . . . but I knew that I would later despise myself if I showed off to someone like Kodai.

'I'm sure you don't know some of the things I know,' she said.

24

'Who cares?' I shrugged, and she smirked mysteriously.

'It's getting dark. Let's go inside.' Kodai and the scent of the flowers were making my head ache.

'Wait for a minute,' she said. 'Do you want to be friends with me?'

'I'm here for only six months – till Amma and Daddy return from Kuwait. They're flying there the day after tomorrow.' I looked carefully at her face in the gathering darkness to see if she was impressed.

' "Daddy" – is that what you call your appa?' Kodai asked. 'It sounds silly.'

I flushed. 'It doesn't.'

'I think it sounds silly,' she insisted.

'I *like* calling him that. I've called him that all my life,' I said.

'My amma says your amma wears silk saris all the time. It's stupid, she says – in this heat,' Kodai said.

It wasn't true. 'Your amma is a fat pig,' I wanted to say, 'and so are you.'

Instead I asked coldly, 'What are these things you know, anyway?'

'I don't know if I should tell you. They are grown-up things.'

'Like?' I felt a sharp thrill of curiosity.

Kodai stepped closer. 'Do you know my brother?' she whispered, her face close to mine, her breath damp on my ear.

I drew back. 'I haven't even seen your brother.'

'His name is Sridhar. He's grown up and goes to college.' She scrutinized my face. 'But he won't like you, I think – not as much as he likes Sudha.'

I looked up.

'He thinks Sudha is beautiful,' Kodai continued.

Other than what Amma had told me, this was the first thing I remember anyone telling me about Sudha – that she was beautiful.

'He once told me that he would like to see her having a bath,' Kodai said. She looked at me seriously. 'Do you want to tell her that when she returns?'

I turned away and walked into the house. The smells of the garden followed me.

'Though he also – sometimes – wishes she were just a *little* plumper,' I heard Kodai wheeze as I walked through the dim pool of orange light flowing out of the kitchen door and went into the house.

*   *   *

Sundar didn't return till late that evening. He didn't work on weekends but had gone to look over the eight acres of land he still owned in Aathur village, which had been rented out in return for a share of the crop. Janaki went upstairs after Kodai left, then came down again to wait for her brother.

'You can eat if you want to,' she told me.

'What about you?'

'I must wait,' she said.

'I'll wait too.'

But by nine o'clock I changed my mind and asked if I could eat. The food tasted just like Amma's cooking though Janaki didn't say a word while serving me. Amma would talk through dinner, asking me questions about school, my teachers and the other girls. Questions I sometimes pretended not to hear. When Sundar came in I had almost finished.

'So you've got our convent-school girl actually

26

sitting on the floor to have her dinner?' he asked.

I thought Janaki looked a little surprised at that. Maybe because Sundar rarely spoke to anyone.

He washed himself and went into the front room to recite his Gayathri. I followed to look at him as he whispered under his breath and touched his forehead, nose and shoulder in silent ritual gestures. My father did this only some evenings when he was not too tired, when he was in the right mood.

I watched Janaki as she moved about quietly serving her brother, watching his plate like an alert bird, making sure he had enough rice and sambhar and vegetables, rice and curd and pickle. She broke the silence only once to ask him something, but he had his head bent over his food and didn't reply. Janaki didn't repeat her question.

*   *   *

The night noises in the house could have been anything. That creak, for instance, could have been the old clock downstairs, or a restless bird, or someone coming softly up the stairs. Janaki's room was completely dark. There was no night lamp, and no street light shone in through the window. My suitcase loomed, a shapeless bulk in the corner. Tomorrow I was to arrange my clothes in the empty shelves in Janaki's large wooden wardrobe. Her saris occupied just one shelf, the topmost one. They were folded neatly and didn't smell of anything. I wondered if the smell I got from Sundar was cigarettes or something else I didn't know. He would be asleep in his room now, probably tired after his journey. The village was nearly fifty miles from Thiruninravur.

27

The small table fan whirred uselessly at my feet. It was a new one because Janaki hadn't had a fan in her room and Amma had said that the heat might be too much for me to take and I might fall ill. I wondered if I could get up and adjust its speed without waking Janaki, who lay on her mattress at the other end of the room, a small quiet mound beneath the thin cotton sheet. My own mattress turned into a ship – it shuddered, creaked, rocked gently down the stairs through the dark front room, nudged the door open and went out past Kodai's house, through the narrow little streets of this town where God once slept.

I heard Amma call out for me as she used to do every evening years ago, when I was still in kindergarten and out at play. *Nithamma . . . Nithi . . . Nithi . . . Nith . . .*

I opened my eyes. The room was still dark but I could see that Janaki was no longer in bed. She was standing up, her back towards me, and looking at herself in the wardrobe mirror.

*   *   *

The first telegram from my parents came four days later. Sundar was in the front room, the morning sunlight bouncing off the little mirror he had propped against a window. I watched his face reflected in fragments – a neat black moustache, long, thick curling eyelashes like a woman's, a cheek lathered with soap, a bead of blood, lips suddenly too red and full on his brown face. The cloth of his veshti was so fine and I could see his long brown legs, covered with curling black hair. I thought he looked mean and menacing, standing there with his legs apart and his head thrown back as he ran the razor carefully across his throat. He'd woken up early that morning, at 5.30, but Janaki had been up even before him to have a bath and to make his coffee.

'Does Sudha also have to get up early every day?' I had asked. They'd told me Sudha was only twenty years old. Surely she needed more sleep than that?

'You've forgotten – Sudha is a priest's daughter. She probably gets up even earlier when she's at home,' Janaki had replied.

When the man from the telegraph office knocked at the door, Janaki stood up to answer it. Neither she nor I had been out of the house since our trip to the railway station.

'Let Nithya open the door,' Sundar said, and Janaki sat down again, her head bent low over a half-shelled heap of green peas on a damp cloth.

'Someone has to sign this, he says,' I called.

Sundar came to the door, wiping his hands impatiently on the towel flung over his shoulder. I watched him open the telegram and waited for him to read it out to us.

'Your amma-appa have reached,' he said shortly, and gave the bit of paper to me.

Reached this morning stop is Nithya doing well stop will write soon stop.

So they were really in Kuwait now. The room was suddenly darker and filled with yellow spots, which floated towards me in a colourless stream that then wedged itself in the middle of my throat as a hard lump. How could they have left me and gone, so far away, with an aunt and uncle I didn't even know or like? As I went up the stairs a thousand people

29

watched me breathlessly as I swept off the stage in a flash of flowing skirts and bare arms. In a minute they would stand up and applaud.

*   *   *

I stayed upstairs till Sundar left for work. Amma had told me that he was the first man in her family to graduate from college. Janaki and Amma had been married while they were still at college. Amma had gone back for her final year after she'd had me. Poor Janaki, of course (she would say), became a widow.

As we ate together, I again marvelled at how young Janaki looked. Was it because she hadn't had children? When she finished cleaning the kitchen she sat down for a moment and leaned against the kitchen wall, her sari wrapped tight around her. Nothing of her could be seen. Not a glimpse of her ankles, not her midriff, not even her arms. Only her wrists and her fine-veined hands as they rested quietly on her lap.

'She looks tired,' I thought. 'Maybe I should have offered to help.' But Janaki told me later that she liked doing the work by herself.

'Let's go out,' I said, feeling restless. Why was she sitting there staring at nothing? 'Let's go for a walk.'

'For a walk?' She looked at me curiously. 'Where will we walk to? And when it is so hot?' Of course – even Amma didn't ever go for a walk without Daddy.

'I'm going upstairs,' she said, just as she had done the same time yesterday and the day before.

But I had something to look forward to that day. Sudha was to return that afternoon. Her father was a priest, Amma had said, and Sudha was the second of his three daughters. He didn't have too much money.

That's why he had agreed to send her to stay with Sundar and Janaki to help with the household chores and the cow. She'd gone home just before Amma and I had arrived. That's why my mother didn't ever get to see Sudha.

'Janaki tells me that Sudha is very young. She should be company for you,' Amma had told me the day before we left Bangalore, as she stood in front of the mirror in our bathroom examining the just-visible strands of grey on her temples. ('Tell me – do I look old? Do you think your Amma is getting *old*?')

Sudha would be back by two in the afternoon, Janaki had said. I decided to wait downstairs. But when the clock struck three, there was still no sign of her. The bus was probably late. I went up to see Janaki but she was fast asleep, her eyelashes resting on the semi-circles of darkness below her eyes. She'd covered herself, as if she were cold. She was a corpse lying there at my feet, small, hard and lifeless. I wondered how she could look *so* different from my mother. Amma's cheeks were round, though her hair was beginning to turn grey; her arms were plump and her stomach was soft and fleshy – like a fruit.

When Sudha came I was waiting for her, sitting on a sack of paddy. She smiled at me and went into her room. She later told me that she hadn't been sure if I would want to talk to her. I waited for her to come out and come downstairs again. When she didn't, I went to stand at her door. She was unpacking her faded canvas bag. The jar of pickle in it had leaked. The tangy smell of mango, chilli powder and oil filled the room. She looked up at me and wrinkled her nose.

'I must have a bath now,' she said, 'I'll be back in ten

minutes.' As she brushed past me she smelt of bus, talcum powder and pickle.

Just when I was thinking of going down, I heard her coming back up the stairs.

'You're still here?' she asked. 'I thought you would be asleep in there.' She gestured towards Janaki's room.

'So you know who I am?' I asked.

'Of course I know who you are.' She seemed surprised. 'They told me you would be here when I got back. You are their sister's daughter.'

I nodded.

'How long are you going to stay?' she asked.

'Six months.'

'You poor child! But don't worry – six months is not such a long time.'

'It is more than one term at St Mary's – that's my school.'

'What a strange way to think of time!'

When Sudha laughed, it rang out loud and clear in the stillness of the afternoon and she clapped her hand across her mouth, raising her eyebrows in half-comic, half-real fear.

'We should be careful,' she said. 'She might wake up, your chitti.'

'But you were the one who laughed – not me.'

'I know. I shouldn't have. Even at home they say that I laugh too loudly. I shouldn't, you know – your chitti doesn't sleep well at night.'

Sudha's mother had given her food, and she hadn't finished it on the bus. She went down to the kitchen to eat it from its soft, plaintain-leaf bundle. She seemed hungry and I wondered if she always got enough to eat while she was at home. But Amma had warned me never to call Sudha a servant. Remember – she is a brahmin girl, an Iyengar just like us.

*   *   *

When Sudha wasn't wearing a sari, when she wore the St Mary's School uniform of knee-length navy-blue skirt and white blouse, she could easily pass as one of the high-school sports prefects whom all the younger girls, except me, had crushes on. She was slender and taller than both Amma and Janaki, and her face was clear and brown and soft. She liked to smile.

Sometimes I sat on the mat in her room watching her dip a finger into a little jar and draw a neat, perfectly round red spot between her brows.

'Let me do it for you, too,' she would say sometimes, and turning around she would hold my chin with her left hand, her lips pouting in fierce concentration. Much later, I gave her a strip of deep-maroon bindis made of felt and plastic.

'They're nice,' Sudha said admiringly, 'but why do you call them bindis? They are *pottus*.'

'It's the Hindi word. It means the same thing.'

'*Bindis*,' she giggled. 'It sounds strange.'

'It's just another language, that's all,' I said sternly.

'Why doesn't my hair grow?' she would sometimes ask, rubbing it fiercely with her handloom towel after a bath. 'I've not cut it since I was a year old, but it doesn't grow.'

Her plait stopped just at her waist, though when she undid it to comb and oil it each strand was strong, black and straight.

'You actually have very nice hair,' she told me, 'like

33

her.' She meant Janaki. 'If only your amma would let it grow.'

She didn't know that most of the girls at my school kept their hair even shorter than mine. That's what I wanted – shoulder-length hair, smartly rubber-banded in a ponytail.

'Maybe I should oil my hair with something else, something special, not coconut oil,' she said. 'But everything else is so expensive!'

'Cut it a bit every fortnight. It will grow double the length you cut off.'

'Are you laughing at me?' She turned around and smiled uncertainly.

'No. That's what one of my classmates says. And she should know – she has really long hair.'

Sudha sighed, twisted her shoulder around and measured her plait in the mirror, which was in her room only because Janaki and Amma had slept there a long time ago.

'Have you ever seen hair under a microscope?' I asked.

'I don't even know what a microscope is.'

'It makes things big. I've seen a grain of sand look as huge as a boulder, and a strand of hair look like a rope.'

'I know what a telescope is,' Sudha said. 'I think I like a telescope better.'

'Why?'

'It brings faraway things closer to you – big things you can't reach. It would be nice to touch the leaves of a coconut tree, the top of the Sri Ranganathaswamy temple – or the moon.'

She stuck her hand out to poke at the moon's silly pink stomach.

*　　　*　　　*

Small, unripe gooseberries lay scattered on the ground around the tree. I counted them as I collected them in my skirt. *Twelve . . . thirteen . . . fourteen . . .* I emptied them in a neat pile on the ground. I now needed salt and chilli powder from the kitchen.

When I sat down, my back against the scratchy bark of the gooseberry tree, the salt had begun to melt, making my hand sticky. I should have brought a plate instead, or a piece of paper.

It was the middle of the morning, Sudha and Janaki were in the house and Sundar was, as usual, at work. In Kuwait it would still be very early in the day, and at St Mary's the sixth-standard girls would be having their Kannada class with Miss Girija. No one would really miss me, and there had been only mild excitement when Miss Joyce had announced that 'Nithya will be away from us for six months, girls. Her parents have got special permission from Sister Principal.'

The teachers would begin to leave out my name when they called from the attendance lists and Latha, the girl who sat next to me in class, would have spread herself out on the bench. The lice in her hair would have nowhere else to go.

It was hot here. It was making me sleepy.

When I woke up, I felt my throat itch. I wondered if the gooseberries were going to give me a cold. Amma didn't ever let me eat raw gooseberries and I wondered if Janaki too would be annoyed. It was difficult to imagine Janaki ever being angry – like Amma sometimes was. Till a few years ago my mother would punish me by pinching the soft flesh beneath my

35

short, little-girl skirts. ('Will you do that again – will you, will you?' her voice high and shivery. Obstinate silence on my part. Or 'Yes, I *will* do it again. *I will, I will* . . .')

My throat was beginning to hurt now and I coughed. It sounded like a small firecracker exploding. A second later another one exploded; someone else was coughing. Leaves rustled somewhere as someone moved. I looked up, but there was no black goblin hanging upside-down from the branches of the gooseberry tree as in the Vikramadithya stories, waiting to jump onto my back and never get off. But there was somebody else close by, probably some boy who'd crept in to steal fruit.

'Hello!' I called loudly.

Whoever it was didn't reply.

'Have you gone?' I asked, more softly this time. Maybe I had frightened him.

Someone moved and the dry twigs snapped beneath his feet. The sound came from behind the row of hibiscus bushes. I ran up to peer through them. At first I thought he was a child or that he was squatting or kneeling down. I then realized that he was only three or four feet tall. His head was too big for his body and he wore black-rimmed spectacles. He looked frightened for a minute and then smiled. It was a strange smile, funny and shy and very sad.

Chapter Two

Sudha started getting excited about the solar eclipse before it even happened.

'Let's go up to my room this evening and get things ready for tomorrow,' she told me the day before. Janaki had asked her to clean Lakshmi's shed that afternoon. I watched her sweep out the damp straw and splash water on the stone floor. She'd already heaped the dung into a basket. The smell of dung was part grass, part milk and part shit. I wrinkled my nose at it.

'Come on,' Sudha said. 'It's only dung. It's not *dirty*!'

'It is. My father says it can lead to terrible things – tetanus, I think.'

Sudha shrugged. 'We plaster our floors with it at home, and none of *us* ever falls ill.'

Lakshmi watched us both with big wet eyes and waited patiently as Sudha got ready to milk her. The man who had come in for the week Sudha was away had been paid off and told that he was no longer needed.

'Poor Raju will miss the two rupees he got every

day,' Sudha sighed, 'but I think Lakshmi likes me better.'

She squatted on the little wooden stool. She had hitched her sari and skirt up to her knees. Her calves were strong and gently muscled, whiter than the gold of her waist and stomach. Her fingers tugged efficiently at Lakshmi's fat pink udders.

'How many sisters and brothers do you have?' I asked, though I already knew. Sudha liked to talk about her family.

'There are three of us and there is my brother – he is fourteen years old. Kausalya, me, Aruna and Ananth.'

It was the beginning of a fairy tale: Once upon a time . . . four children poor but good, in a little cottage. And sometime, somehow they would be rich, good *and* happy.

'Wouldn't you like to go back home?' I asked.

'I got back here *yesterday* – I can't think of going back now!'

'Yes, but wouldn't you like to be with your family?'

'It can't be helped,' she said simply. 'We need the money.'

'Why didn't they send Kausalya instead? Isn't she the one older than you?'

'She is not as strong as I am. And anyway Amma is beginning to worry about her marriage.'

'And your father – isn't he worried about it?'

'Oh, poor Appa is worried about *hundreds* of things,' she said sadly.

And that's what Sudha's father remained to me for the rest of my life even after I met him – a shadowy little man, crushed by the things that happened to him.

Lakshmi's milk was white and foamy in the bucket. Later in the evening the kitchen would smell of boiling milk. And the two families who bought milk and curd from here would send their children over to the door with clean vessels. But I thought that it would be more fun to be like Krishna, who'd put his plump baby's lips around a cow's udders and felt the milk squirt warm and fresh into his mouth.

'What are you thinking about?' Sudha smiled.

'Nothing. Tell me – what do you do at home in the evenings?'

'I help with the housework and we eat very early.' Talking of home seemed to make her sad, but when she spoke again she was smiling.

'Even now my amma sometimes makes the four of us sit round her and then feeds us. There are fewer plates to wash that way, she says.'

'She feeds even Ananth?'

'Ananth is the baby of the house,' Sudha laughed.

'And will he become a priest like your father?'

'Oh, no! We want him to finish his SSLC and go to college. If he's lucky he'll get a job in a government office. But they say it's very difficult with all this reservation and everything.' She looked anxiously at me. 'What do you think?' she asked.

'I don't know. Maybe it is.'

Lakshmi absent-mindedly flicked her tail against Sudha's face.

'Ay! Don't do that!' she cried, and Lakshmi looked at her in surprise. Her tail had left a streak of dung on Sudha's cheek.

'Come on, touch her,' Sudha urged me. 'She won't mind.'

'Someone told me cows don't like being touched when they're being milked.'

'Oh, Nithya! Lakshmi is not a *cow* – she's a *buffalo*!'

But I preferred to stand by the door and watch.

Someone came up behind me. I knew it wasn't Janaki so I looked back. Sundar must have come to wash himself after he came home from work, and wondered at the sound of our voices. He was watching Sudha through the soft darkness of the cowshed. He didn't even seem to notice me. I saw that he looked a little – puzzled. But when I looked back again after a couple of minutes he had gone. He had moved so softly that Sudha hadn't even realized he had been there.

That night she and I smoked square bits of glass over a kerosene lamp in her room. 'We'll both be blind this time tomorrow,' I said.

'Why?'

'That's what looking at a solar eclipse does to you.'

'I've heard people say that. But is it true?'

'I don't know. But one of the girls in my class pretended to be blind one day after a solar eclipse.'

'Why?' Sudha looked up from her piece of glass, startled.

'She hadn't done her homework. She had to think of something to tell them.'

'Couldn't she just say she had a *stomach ache* or something?'

'I once pretended I had sprained my leg because I didn't want to play hockey.'

It was fun telling Sudha these stories. I liked to talk about school and I liked to watch her laugh. We didn't hear Janaki coming into the room.

'My brother is trying to sleep,' she said to Sudha. She wasn't angry; her voice hadn't changed even a little. 'And remember, you have to be up early, too.'

Sudha had stood up when Janaki had come in. After she left, she put the lamp and the pieces of glass away. Her face was flushed and she looked troubled. I wondered if Sundar had been disturbed and had sent Janaki to speak to us.

The next morning we went out to the garden to watch the sun being swallowed, slowly and leisurely, in all his fire and splendour by Kethu the giant snake. The white disc turned to yellow to orange to coppery-red and then disappeared. The garden took the shapes and shadows of the night for the short minute before it became morning again.

'The silly birds were actually beginning to fly back to their nests!' Sudha said, laughing. She looked at me. 'What's the matter? Why are you so quiet?' she asked anxiously.

'I haven't had anything to eat ever since I woke up,' I said. I was beginning to feel bad-tempered with hunger.

'You can't eat before an eclipse – you know that,' Sudha said, stroking my hair tenderly. 'But it's over now. Go and have your bath – I'll place dharba grass on all the vessels in the kitchen and then get your food ready.'

I had had one bath already and didn't want to have a second one. And it was really only the stupid sun being blocked from the earth by the moon.

*   *   *

When Janaki had her periods she would stay in the little room next to Sudha's till the fifth day. I went in to look at her.

'Do you need something?' she asked.

She looked just the same as she did any other day. Amma would sometimes complain that her back hurt, or she would snap at us and be irritable. But my father had said that there was no need for her to sit apart.

'I don't care if they insist on it at your mother's house,' he'd say. 'I don't see why you should stay shut up all by yourself.'

Amma had told me that that had taken her a while to get used to. And even now she wouldn't go near the gods in the kitchen, and tried to avoid touching my father when she sat behind him on the scooter, till she'd washed her hair on the fourth day.

'Where's my sister?' Sundar asked as Sudha served his food that night.

'She can't come down,' I said, and he understood and didn't ask any more questions.

A banana had been taken up to Janaki. I wanted Sundar to finish his dinner and go upstairs quickly so that Sudha and I could begin eating, though she might want to serve me first. But Sundar asked for a second helping of nearly everything that night, and ate infuriatingly slowly. Whenever Sudha bent to serve him, I could smell whatever she had washed her hair with. I knew that Sundar could smell it, too. I saw his eyes following her when she walked into the kitchen to fetch things. But he didn't look up at her or speak.

*　　*　　*

I had already seen Kodai's brother Sridhar in their garden. He was thin, like his father, and impossibly slender-waisted. A giraffe. Or perhaps a deer. Sudha had told me that though he didn't look like he was capable of anything at all, Sridhar was celebrated on the street as a 'rank student' and was now in the missionary college at Arani studying physics. He had wanted to go to a college in Madras but his father said it would be far too expensive.

I was looking into the well in Sundar's garden. I'd not seen too many wells before and never such a deep one. It was a round shaft of night descending deep into nothingness. I opened my eyes wide as I could but I couldn't see the glimmer of water, and when I dropped a pebble in I barely heard the splash.

'Hallo!' I called to the darkness, but got no reply. And then: 'Lo . . . lo . . .' someone called back in a deep mournful voice.

If anyone wanted to die, the simplest, most certain way would be to clamber onto the stone wall and slip softly into the darkness.

Long ago my grandmother's nose ring had slipped into this well but no one would agree to get in and look for it. She had never quite stopped thinking about it, and according to Amma she would insist on taking reluctant guests to the garden and getting them to look inside the well. Maybe she felt that someone with miraculously sharp vision would be able to see the piece, glimmering like an angry red eye deep in the water.

Sridhar squeezed through a gap in the hibiscus and came to stand near the well not far from me. There was nothing unusual about that. Though I had not seen

43

Janaki or Sundar or Sudha go into their neighbours' garden, I knew that Kodai would come to pick gooseberries or a raw mango that her sharp eyes had glimpsed lying on the ground, and Kamala would come to take the clothes that had blown across from her clothesline. Or to smell whatever was being cooked or to see if she could hear some interesting snatches of conversation. Maybe she hoped that one day, if she was lucky, she would discover something exciting happening in this infuriatingly quiet household.

Sridhar stood a couple of feet away from me, and when he looked up I wondered if he was shortsighted. I remembered what his sister had said about him and I stared back. That seemed to disconcert him. He looked away and then looked at me again. A squirrel burst into a hysterical cry somewhere. Maybe a cat or a crow had got after it. I went to investigate. When I got back Sridhar was still there. His fingers drummed on the stone wall in nervous secret code. The sound of chanting rumbled and slurred through the old microphone in the Hanuman temple two streets away.

'Why don't they shut up?' Sridhar asked, leaning towards me.

'Who?'

'They.' He jerked his long neck in the direction of the temple.

'Why – you don't like it?'

'No,' he said sadly, and looked into the well. 'I wonder where this leads to,' he said after a while. He sounded troubled. 'Do you think it leads to Hell?'

'Maybe not that far,' I said.

'Do you believe in Hell? Or in Heaven for that matter? And in . . . all that?'

44

I shrugged. He had lost the first few buttons of his shirt – it gaped open to reveal his smooth pale chest and his sacred thread, brown with sweat and dirt.

'Come on – you haven't told me yet – do you or don't you believe?' he asked fiercely.

I didn't reply because I didn't know. And I didn't want to talk about it anyway. I wanted to be alone that morning. But he spoke again, this time very gently.

'I feel the time has come for me to reexamine everything, the way I've lived and what I've believed in especially.' He was beginning to sound agitated now. 'But I – I don't know – I feel I'm getting nowhere.'

'Have the Christian priests in your college been talking to you?' I asked.

'Oh, no – they are very careful about these things. They don't say a word. *I've* been trying to work things out for myself because I'm sick – of all this.' He jerked his shoulder towards his garden, his parents, his house, the Hanuman temple and the small dusty world that was the only one he had known.

'But I sometimes think I don't deserve anything better,' he continued.

'Why not?'

He looked at me in surprise, as though the answer was really so simple. 'Because I am a coward, was never brave enough to do anything about anything.'

I waited for him to say more but he only stood next to me, his eyes fixed on the ground. A big rust-coloured ant crawled up the faded cotton of his trouser leg. If it tried hard enough it could slip below his shirt and reach bare flesh. But when Sridhar shifted it fell down and lay on the ground, its small spindly legs kicking indignantly at the sky.

45

It looked like he had finished for the morning. I turned to go in. I wondered what Janaki had told Sudha to cook for the day. I was beginning to be very interested in food all of a sudden. I was slightly ashamed of it and made certain that no one else found out.

'Listen,' Sridhar called out after me when I was already halfway to the kitchen door. He sounded like his repulsive little sister. He strode towards me, one hand thrust into his pocket, and bent clumsily to look at my face.

'Sudha – who stays with you – is she ever – lonely?' His voice had sunk to a whisper. I stared back at him, expressionless.

'She is so beautiful, isn't she?' he asked urgently. 'Tell her that from me. Tell her that I think she's very beautiful.'

I turned and walked steadily into the house, but before pushing open the door I looked back. Sridhar was standing where I had left him, looking up at the hot sky, his face twisted as if he was in pain.

That night I dreamt I was a nun – a cloistered Carmelite maybe – with the days and nights falling gently and noiselessly behind me like leaves. The neat veiled shadows of Sudha, Janaki and Amma were all around me. Their lives too were beautiful and un-complicated, and I knew that if it wasn't so dark I would have been able to see that their faces were radiant with peace.

*　　　*　　　*

Ambuja Pati, Kodai's and Sridhar's grandmother and Vasu's mother, lived with them. The first time I saw

46

her was when I went to ask that a copy of the *Hindu* that Sridhar had borrowed from Sundar be returned. I went through the back of the house. Kodai's garden had fewer trees than Sundar's and they didn't own a cow, though Vasu had a shed where he reared pigeons. This was thought of as an unclean pastime, but as far as I ever knew it was Vasu's single gesture of defiance of the world. As I passed the shed I reminded myself that I still had to go in and look at the birds.

Kamala didn't know where the newspaper was. She cleared a pile of unfolded clothes from a rickety plastic chair to check, reached up to run her hands over the dusty top of a cupboard and then stomped heavily into the kitchen.

'Sridhar must have left it here,' she said as she came out, triumphantly waving it at me.

'Stay, stay and eat something,' she urged. 'And tell me how you are spending your holiday. Are you very lonely . . . ?' Her eyes glinted with curiosity.

'No, I have to go now. Sundar is waiting for the newspaper.'

She followed me into the front room.

'Who is this child?' Ambuja Pati asked from her corner. She nearly always sat there, I later discovered, away from the light, like an ancient night bird.

'Who is this child?' she repeated. She swooped out of the corner and looked me up and down like Kodai had, especially at the skirt that didn't quite reach my ankles.

'Oh, this is Padma's – Sundar and Janaki's sister's – daughter. Her name is Nithya.' Kamala fluttered around her mother-in-law nervously. 'Don't you remember, I was telling you that her amma and appa . . .'

47

'I remember,' Ambuja Pati cut her short. 'I haven't yet grown that old.'

'Oh, no, of course not!' Kamala beamed. 'Amma has a very good memory,' she told me proudly.

I stared at Ambuja Pati. Sudha had told me that she had been a widow ever since she was seventeen years old. She didn't wear a blouse, I noticed, and her white sari had slipped off to reveal grey stubble and a scalp dry and leathery after being shaven a thousand times.

'Why doesn't Janaki come and visit me any more?' she asked me.

Ask her yourself. How am I supposed to know?

'So your parents have gone somewhere?' Her voice was loud and clear and barely trembled. I nodded.

'You must be bored living here – this is not like Madras or your Bangalore.'

I shook my head. Ambuja Pati turned to Kamala.

'The child can't speak or what?' Her eyes flashed irritably. 'Or is she just being stubborn?' She then smiled grimly and began to hobble out of the room, her bony shoulders hunched. 'Tell Janaki to visit me soon. I haven't seen her for a long time,' she stopped to tell me. I saw that she didn't let an inch of wrinkled stomach or withered breast show between the scanty folds of her sari.

Sudha had told me that Ambuja Pati was eighty years old. She'd been married to Vasu's father when she was eleven, and had come to live in this house. 'Vasu's father died just after he was born, and she brought him up all on her own – though it wasn't as if there was no money or anything. Think of that – sixty-nine years ago!' Sudha had said.

Sudha was overwhelmed by any length of time

48

longer than twenty years. The Indus Valley civilization is 5,000 years old, I liked to tell her, and it is nearly 2,000 years since the birth of Christ, and the British left 39 years ago. Her eyes would widen.

'Do they like Ambuja Pati?' I asked. 'Do Kodai and Sridhar and the rest of them?'

'I don't know,' she said. 'But she still runs that house. Kamala can't spend a rupee without letting her mother-in-law know.'

'But Vasu has pigeons in his garden. Surely his mother wouldn't like that?' I argued.

'She hates the birds. She will go nowhere near them if she can help it, and threatens to give them away every other day. I'm sure she *will* give them away very soon.'

'But does her family *like* her?'

'She's very religious and orthodox. You saw the clothes she wears – she's been like that since her husband died. And she eats only one meal a day – and nothing cooked even then. She doesn't ever leave the house – she wouldn't even go to her own son's wedding.'

'So do *you* like her?'

Sudha simply said, 'I think she is a great lady.'

I didn't know what to say to that. But I didn't give Janaki Ambuja Pati's message. Two days after my visit Sundar, who was leaving for work, told her, 'I saw Vasu yesterday evening. He told me that his mother wants you to go and visit her.' Janaki was watering the front steps and didn't look up.

'You should spend more time with her,' Sundar said. We both watched him start his scooter and splutter off down the road.

Janaki came downstairs earlier than usual that afternoon. I could hear her working at the pump, and after a few minutes she came in rubbing her face dry with the end of her sari. Her eyes were just slightly swollen with sleep, the coarseness of the towel made her face look flushed and her hair was disheveled. She looked sad, young and very lovely. She stopped to get herself a drink of water from the pot in the kitchen.

'Do you want to come with me to Kamala's house?' she asked without looking at me.

Janaki had never asked me to go with her anywhere before. She liked being by herself. I didn't reply.

'So you don't want to come?' she asked, turning around.

I knew that if I said I didn't she wouldn't try to persuade me, as Amma would have done.

'I'll come with you,' I said, though I didn't want Janaki to visit Ambuja Pati.

I washed my face and let Sudha plait my hair. As I stepped out of the house I could smell the soap I'd used. Janaki had combed her hair severely over her forehead and behind her ears. Her ears, neck and wrists were bare.

'So you have come at last!' Ambuja Pati exclaimed when we entered. She had been waiting for us. She was sitting on the floor, stringing jasmine buds on a length of wet plantain fibre. 'Sit where I can see you,' she ordered, and both of us sat on the floor in front of her. 'So how have you been?' she asked Janaki. 'And how is your brother?'

Her eyes were sharper than usual that evening. A reptile on its way to becoming the first leathery scaled bird.

Kamala lowered herself on the floor next to me. Vasu hadn't yet got back from work and Sridhar was still at college, she said. And Kodai, who had eaten nearly a dozen custard apples the night before, was ill.

'He brought home two dozen,' Kamala said. She meant her husband. 'The typist in his office has a tree in his compound.' Vasu worked at Arani railway station, fifteen miles outside Thiruninravur. So Kodai had eaten over a dozen not-quite-ripe custard apples, making tireless expeditions to the sacks of rice in which her mother had stored them. 'And she's been ill the whole morning,' Kamala said worriedly. 'It looks like she ate the fruit and skin and everything. Because when she vomited . . .'

'That girl's greedy,' Ambuja Pati cut her short. 'And too fat.'

'That's not her fault, the poor thing. She's taken after me,' Kamala said apologetically.

I wondered if they'd send me to sit with Kodai. I would refuse if they asked me to. Janaki shouldn't be left alone. I looked at her sitting stiff and upright as Kamala and her mother-in-law talked. I couldn't guess if she was even listening to them.

'Sridhar?' Kodai had wandered into the room, her usually firm body sagging a little. She stopped in surprise when she saw us.

'Sridhar is not at home?' she whined.

'Tell me – when does that brother of yours ever get home before dark?' her grandmother asked impatiently. 'And as for you – why don't you just go to sleep?'

Kodai turned away from us and went in. Kamala heaved herself up and followed her. We watched them go.

'And then?' Ambuja Pati asked, looking at Janaki sharply. 'What else is happening?'

'What else can happen?' Janaki said. 'Nithya is staying with us – but you know about that already.'

She wasn't looking at Ambuja Pati. She had fastened her eyes on the pale-blue wall behind her head. There was a picture of a small dark blur against a brown background on the wall above her head. I later learnt that it was a photograph of Ambuja Pati's husband.

'So you are beginning to feel tired?' Ambuja Pati asked.

Janaki didn't reply.

'And how old are you? Thirty-four? Thirty-five?'

'Thirty-four.'

That was five years younger than Amma. I didn't know if that made Janaki young or old.

'And I am eighty.' Ambuja Pati threw her head back and laughed. 'Sometimes I can't believe it myself. Eighty years old!'

Her fit of mirth made her wheeze and choke, and Janaki got up to get her water. She shook her head – she wanted Janaki to stay where she was.

'Do you still eat at night?' she asked.

'Sometimes.'

'And you've still got your hair, your nice long plait. And a brother to look after you.' She reached out to touch Janaki's hair with one brittle hand, as if she needed to feel its softness. Her grey eyes were suddenly gentle. Janaki drew back very slightly and Ambuja Pati let her hand fall. They didn't look at each other.

'They all think women like us are cursed,' Ambuja Pati continued, 'but you will realize that finally – this

52

is better.' She looked at Janaki and weighed her words carefully before she spoke next.

'You don't believe me, do you – when I tell you that? That this is better?'

Janaki shrugged.

'But you should have realized it yourself by now – you are not so young any more,' the old lady said.

Janaki's slim shoulders slumped under their burden of thirty-four years.

Let's go home. I wanted to tug at her sari as I would at Amma's years ago at the movie theatre, at a sari store . . . *Let's go home, Amma . . . Isn't it time we went home . . . ?*

But they both seemed to have forgotten that I was there. We could hear Kodai being loudly sick inside, throwing up white curdled custard apple, and her mother saying that if this continued much longer they'd have to go the clinic.

'I look at Kamala sometimes,' Ambuja Pati was saying, 'and I am disgusted. She eats too much, for one thing. And she's still interested in what kind of sari she can buy for Deepavali, at the age of forty-five, and sometimes, at night even now . . .'

Janaki looked away quickly.

'The thing is to live without desire,' the old lady said. Her voice was almost tender, as if she were talking to a confused child whom she loved. 'To be grateful that Sri Narayana has given us the opportunity to learn to live without desire.'

'I don't desire anything.'

I looked up at that – Janaki's voice was harsh, almost angry.

'Don't you?' Ambuja Pati's sly knowing smile ironed out the wrinkles on her face and lips.

Kamala came in to say that Kodai had fallen asleep at last, and to wonder why Sridhar still hadn't come home. After a few minutes Janaki said that we had to leave.

'And before you go,' Ambuja Pati was no longer smiling, 'there's just one more thing. Get your sister's daughter to wear long skirts.'

'What does it matter? Nithya is only a child,' Janaki said.

'Kamala tells me that she is nearly eleven years old,' Ambuja Pati said. She looked as if she expected Janaki to argue, but Janaki remained silent.

Ambuja Pati had finished stringing the jasmine, and before we left she gave Kamala three strands of it – one for Kamala, one for Kodai, and one for me. Though the flowers smelt cool and fresh when Kamala tucked them into my plait, I decided I would pull them off once I got home, and throw them out of the kitchen door. But I forgot, and when I woke up the next morning I found jasmine petals, brown and curling at the edges, scattered over my sheet and pillow.

Janaki walked ahead, and it was only when we got into our own house that I noticed her face had suddenly got thinner and even more pale. She ignored Sudha when she asked her if she wanted to eat anything, and we watched her go up the stairs slowly. The visit had tired her out. There was really no need for her to have gone to see Ambuja Pati that evening.

*   *   *

54

'Go and ask Janaki if we can remove the snake-gourd creeper from the garden,' Sudha told me. She squatted near the pump rinsing out vessels. I sat on the washing stone watching her.

'Are there no more gourds on it?' Janaki asked me.

'Sudha said the plant is dead. She wants to plant a pumpkin creeper instead. She says Sundar likes pumpkin.'

'I think we needn't worry about that till much later,' Janaki said quietly.

'But can we remove the snake-gourd creeper today?'

I didn't care about much later; I would be back home then. But removing the snake-gourd plant would give me something to do that afternoon.

'Yes, you can. But I don't understand why you want to stay out when it's so hot.'

The afternoon sun filtered through the canopy of the tamarind tree as Sudha and I bent over the creeper. It was at the farthest end of the garden and had grown completely wild. The dark-green star-shaped leaves had turned brown, and the curling tendrils and the stem against which you could bruise your hand when it was green had become brittle twigs and twisted cords of yellow rope. Sudha had brought along a basket and two old knives that smelt of mud and cold metal. The dry leaves tickled the soles of our feet.

The creeper had served them well for many months, Sudha said. Though they'd sent dozens of snake gourds to the neighbours, sometimes to the people at Sundar's office, she had had to chop snake gourd every other day for lunch. It had made her fingers smell green, fresh and bitter, even after she washed them.

It was nice to keep Sudha talking. The garden was

too still with only the sound of the wind and Lakshmi sometimes shifting in her shed.

'What is your favorite vegetable?' I asked. Sometimes, in school, during Moral Science class, my classmates and I would talk about food in ravenous whispers while the teacher sat at her table writing letters.

'Brinjal,' Sudha said.

'Brinjal looks like fried fish,' I said. She was appalled.

'And boiled yam looks like meat – like beef, actually.'

'Don't!' She straightened up, her face wrinkled with disgust. 'How can you even *talk* about these things?'

'I've seen all kinds of food in my friends' lunch boxes at school,' I said proudly. Sudha shuddered.

It took us two hours to cut down the creeper and gather its remains in our baskets. The ground over which it had spread now looked bare, soft and sad.

'We'll plant the pumpkin seeds I brought from home next week,' Sudha said comfortingly. 'Your Sundar Mama will like that.'

'Will he?' I was tired. Sweat poured down the sides of my face and I felt dirty. 'I don't care. I need to have a bath right away.'

'Go ahead. I can empty the baskets.'

I was inside the house rubbing coconut oil on my arms and feet after my bath when she came in.

'What's happened to you?' I asked. Her face had broken into fiery red spots.

'I've been bitten by something.'

She too had a bath but it didn't help. The blotches spread down her face and up her arms before breaking out on the bare strip of her midriff. The skin on her

56

calves, when she lifted up the hem of her sari to show me, was red and swollen.

'Caterpillars!' I guessed.

I had seen a blanket of furry black worms layer the bark of the drumstick tree. Even the thought of them made me shiver.

'Or a spider,' Sudha said, scratching her throat. She left a purple-red band on the inflamed skin.

'Don't do that,' I begged. 'It makes it worse.'

'But I can't stop!' She seemed frightened. 'Do you think it could have been poisonous?'

I felt helpless. 'Do you think we should call Janaki?'

'No.'

'Let's wait for Sundar, then.'

So we waited for him. But when he came home the itchiness had worn off and the blotches had turned from red to purple to tiny light-pink spots.

'What's happened?' he asked. So he had noticed, though I hadn't seen him looking up at either of us when he came in.

Sudha remained silent.

'She's been bitten by something,' I said. 'We thought it was poisonous.' I looked carefully at him.

'But I'm already feeling better,' Sudha said, smiling nervously.

Sundar switched on the light. 'Turn your face that way,' he told her. She stood with her back against the wall.

'I don't think it's anything we need to worry about,' he said, looking carefully down at her. 'But some lime paste might help. Janaki has some in the kitchen with the betal leaves,' he said, turning to me.

'It looks like it was some kind of spider,' he was

saying when I came back with the container of lime. His voice sounded strange, and he raised his hand to touch Sudha's cheek. 'I'll give you an Avil. It will make you sleepy, but you'll be fine by morning.'

The tips of his fingers must have been cool against her hot skin.

*   *   *

Some days after that, two sacks of fresh green chillies were crushed by a passing tractor in front of the house. They must have fallen off the back of one of the lorries that sometimes preferred to take this road, which was, in spite of its gravel-and-sand surface, better than the pothole-marked main road. The wet, pungent odour drew a crowd into the street. Even Ambuja Pati was there holding a cloth over her nose and mouth, shading her eyes against the sun. Everyone spluttered and sneezed over the broken stalks, torn chilli flesh and crushed white seeds. I felt my nostrils burn and my eyes water. Some of the men had fetched buckets of water and brooms to clear the road. There was Narayan Mama, who had taught English at the local government college for thirty years but turned both anti-English *and* anti-Tamil after retirement. He believed that Sanskrit was the solution to India's linguistic problems. He went to Madras a couple of times every year to meet with groups that worked for the preservation of Sanskrit, the preservation of our 4,000-year-old tradition, the preservation of a glorious Hindu past. Narayan Mama had a vision of the world as one big salt-crusted, cast-iron jar of pickles, and was respected by everyone who knew him in Thiruninravur.

Gopal, who worked quietly and without fuss next to Sundar, had almost no money and too many children and had had his sacred thread snapped off when he was younger, one unruly day during the protest movements of the '60s. Everyone knew that his wife, Bhagya, wore bangles of artificial gold because she had given away all the jewellery she had brought from her mother's house to her two older daughters on their wedding days. Even her thali hung on a plain yellow thread around her neck.

But star-shaped diamond earrings still glittered on Sulochana, who lived across the street from Bhagya. She had once entered a recipe contest and won a pressure cooker. Her husband, Seshadri, who also worked in Sundar's office, had bragged about this for a while, though he'd always added that he still thought his mother was a better cook. And Seshadri didn't let Sulochana *use* the pressure cooker, saying that rice and vegetables were tastier when boiled the old-fashioned way. Seshadri was an expert on the weather. Sudha, who stood next to me giving a whispered account of all that she knew of Sundar's neighbours, said that he had maintained records of the temperatures in this district for the last fifteen years.

A crowd of little boys hopped around in faded shorts and undershirts till one or two of them were smacked by their parents and told to keep out of the way. Many of them had severely cropped hair, because they went to the Catholic school attached to Sridhar's college and the Jesuit fathers said that they didn't encourage hippies or vagabonds.

'I am soon going to organize a group and teach our boys Vishnusahasranamam and Ashtalakshmistrotram,'

Narayan Mama was saying loudly. He was worried they would grow up to be careless young men who might or might not recite the Gayathri every day, whose sacred threads would get grimy and discoloured around their chests till they were reminded to change them only once a year, during Avani Attam. The girls stayed closer to their front steps, neat and pretty in flowered cotton skirts and oiled plaits.

Nearly everyone was out except the very old (though no one was – no one could be – older than Ambuja Pati), the very ill, those who had to stay inside because they couldn't risk their neighbours finding out that they hadn't yet had a bath, women who had their periods and Janaki.

Sridhar leaned against his front gate and watched the crowds with brooding eyes, looking bored and exhausted. He didn't talk to anyone or go forward to help the other men till someone called, 'Hey, Cheedu! Come on here! Since when have you become too important to join us?'

Kodai, who had been standing near her brother, came up to Sudha and me. Did she possess an invisible set of antennae, I wondered, that drew her to wherever I happened to be? She must have recovered from the custard-apple mishap.

'You saw the green chillies on the road?' she asked me, wide-eyed with wonder. I didn't bother to reply.

'I sat on a red chilli once,' she continued, 'though there was a mat between it and me.'

'What happened?' Sudha giggled.

'I was talking to Nithya,' Kodai said sullenly.

But Sudha didn't hear her. Sundar was signalling to

her to bring another broom from inside the house. Kodai waited till she had gone.

'It was terrible,' she said.

'What was?' I didn't want to hear about her encounter with the red chilli, and tried to sound as rude as I possibly could.

Kodai actually looked a little hurt, and turned away. But she sidled towards me again after a few minutes.

'Do you know that man?' she whispered. I recognized him at once. He was the little man I'd seen that afternoon three weeks ago when I was half asleep beneath the gooseberry tree.

'I've seen him before,' I whispered back.

'Where?' Her eyes narrowed with interest.

'Behind our house.'

'I thought so,' Kodai nodded knowingly. 'He's there a lot of the time. His name is Raghu.'

He was standing at the fringes of the crowd. No one paid much attention to him and he watched the scene quietly, peering between the long tree-trunks of other men's legs. He didn't offer to help and no one asked him to. Though he was very short, his shoulders and chest were broad, and his little legs in brown khaki trousers were sturdy and muscular. He had a shock of thick black hair on his oversized head, and below his old-fashioned spectacles his nose and mouth were thick and fleshy. He seemed to realize that Kodai and I were talking about him, and he smiled at us uncertainly.

'Does he live here – on this street?' I asked.

'Oh, no, he wouldn't live here. He's not even a *proper* brahmin, you know.'

Kodai's mother had told her that Raghu's father

belonged to GC Street but had been a restless man who had left home and wandered all over the country before coming back to Thiruninravur. He had then had an affair with Raghu's mother, a woman from the goldsmith caste who had a reputation for wildness and was a disgrace to her family. Raghu's father had died almost immediately after he was born, so Raghu had always lived among his mother's people. Everyone knew that his deformity was a result of his parents' wrongdoings.

In half an hour the mess had been neatly cleared away, leaving the street wet and muddy. People were beginning to drift back into their houses and Sridhar was hurrying into his, blind with pain – he had got his hands covered with invisible chilli juice and then absent-mindedly rubbed his eyes and a broken pimple on his cheek.

Raghu was still there. He was nodding and gesticulating to Kodai – it looked like he wanted her to go back into the house.

'He wants to talk to you,' I said.

'Oh, he just wants to see me in the garden,' Kodai said.

'Why?'

Kodai stared at me. 'Oh, so you don't know yet?'

She waddled into the house, pushing the gate open with a plump shoulder. 'Come with me if you want to,' she said. 'I'm sure he'd like to meet you because . . .'

I hurried towards her. Some of the neighbours still lingered in small groups and I didn't want anyone who happened to be close enough to overhear whatever Kodai had to say.

'. . . because he's interested in anyone who has

anything to do with Janaki,' she said. 'They were at college together, the year Janaki spent in college before she got married. Maybe you'll be able to tell him more about her.'

I froze, my hand on the latch. 'I'm not coming,' I said. I went to stand just inside Sundar's gate. The street was almost empty now, and in a while Sudha came out and called me in for lunch.

'Don't bother me. I'll come when I'm hungry,' I replied.

When I did go in, I walked straight through the kitchen where the three of them were and went into the garden. It was cool after the street. The air was heavy with the buzz of insects, one of which had bitten Sudha. I remembered the rawness of her skin and how she'd looked up at Sundar, her eyes wide with wonder and a little bit of fear. She'd probably want me to come in soon and help her while the afternoon away.

Everyone in Kodai's house seemed to be inside too, eating or having their afternoon naps. I walked quietly to the rows of bushes, but there was no little man there asking questions about Janaki.

I didn't talk to Sudha for the rest of the day. I insisted on staying in Janaki's room. I had a headache, I said, and Janaki gave me a pill but didn't force me to take it when I refused.

'Tell me if you begin to feel worse,' she said, and turned to the pile of Sundar's clothes she was ironing.

I buried my head in my pillow and remembered Raghu's shy eyes, his grotesque little body and his hopeful smile. Though I drifted off to sleep and slept through the afternoon, I woke up feeling exhausted.

When I came back upstairs after dinner I saw Sundar sitting with Janaki. He didn't do that too often and I wondered why he had come. He was telling her about problems he was having with the man who cultivated their fields and wondering if he should take leave from work for their second cousin's daughter's wedding in Madras next week. Janaki said very little though I knew that she was listening. Sundar seemed nervous, as if something was troubling him. He got up abruptly and left the room soon.

I looked at Janaki and wondered at how calm she was that evening. Happy because her brother had spent time with her? At peace with herself because she had made up her mind to live a life without any need or hope? It irritated me. I wanted to remind her of how she had looked after that conversation with Ambuja Pati and of the anger that had seemed to batter her that night, making the trees in the garden and the walls of the house seem thick and impenetrable and this room seem small and close.

Chapter Three

Evenings in Sundar's house were long and still. Even
Sudha would be busy, and I would wander out into
the garden where no leaves stirred – it seemed to be
holding its breath and waiting. It was at times like this
that I began missing home.

It was never as quiet in Bangalore in the evenings.
Vendors selling vegetables and fruit walked up and
down our street, pushing their carts till after sunset,
and the voices of the smaller children, playing in the
marigold-bordered park under the watchful eyes of the
mali, floated up to the house. The mali never let them
go near his flowers but washed their bruised knees
and elbows at the tap near his room and intervened
in the quarrels that erupted without warning, separat-
ing the little boys who kicked and bit each other, fused
into fierce dusty bundles rolling on the grass.

The older boys played loud unruly cricket in the
street, some of them already very aware of the girls
perched on the compound walls watching them.
Keshav Reddy, Deepa K.S., Abdul Wahab, Ravi Paul,

Shylini and Kevin D'Souza. I used to play 'dark-room' with them in Kevin's house till some time ago. Because his mother was a typist and usually worked late and his father played drums at a hotel, his house was often our own to run wild in. It was hot and dark and lovely and mysterious hiding beneath his parents' bed, between the trunk full of old copies of Christian magazines with the pale, soft-eyed face of the boy-saint Dominic Savio on their covers and the wooden box where the table-fan was kept after summer. I had once hidden in Kevin's mother's cupboard and marvelled at the softness and scent of the little dresses she wore, but had still been relieved that my own amma always, *always* wore a sari.

While they'd been building an extra room in Keshav's house three years ago, I had joined the others in leaping off the neighbouring parapet into the pile of sand heaped against the wall. It had not been a very high fall, but my heart had thumped wildly each time I had crouched on the parapet and got ready to jump. The cool evening breeze had rushed in my ears as I descended. One of the boys who had been too scared to do it had been coaxed up the parapet. 'Go on!' the rest of us had mocked. 'Scaredy-pot!' He'd fallen down with a ragged cry, and when he staggered out of the sand pile there was sand in his eyes and his upper lip was bleeding because he had struck his face against his knee.

After a while I stopped going out in the evenings but Amma, tired of washing clothes, cooking and listening to film songs on the radio all by herself the whole day, still celebrated my father's return. She liked to switch on the lights in all the rooms.

66

'Like Deepavali every day,' she would say, laughing guiltily, thinking of the electricity bills. She liked to get us all together to tell her what had happened through the day.

'I'm not coming,' I would say, more and more often in the last one or two years. 'You may not have homework to think about but I do.'

Inside my room, with my books open before me just in case one of my parents came in, I would listen to the sound of their voices as low and steady as a distant waterfall.

I knew that my father didn't approve of me spending the evenings by myself. I heard him asking Amma why I was alone so much of the time. Why didn't I go out and play with the other little girls in the neighbourhood?

'She's not a *little* girl any more,' Amma had once said.

'That's the point. No ten-year-old likes to be alone.'

'Nithya is different.' Amma had also begun to sound a bit worried. 'I think she's the only one here who doesn't have a really close friend.'

She was right. All the other girls had 'best friends'. They gave each other cards made of unruled white paper torn out of geometry notebooks and pressed flowers, talked in whispers in class and cried when the teacher discovered they were best friends and made them sit apart. They also wrote letters to each other in sealed inlands during the summer holidays when their parents took them out of town, holidays that would have been perfect if only they could have been together.

I shuddered at the thought of a best friend. Someday

Amma and Appa would understand that I was best left alone.

From the window of my room, after sunset when the street was empty, I would watch Meena and Suresh, who were much older than any of us and went to college, come out of their houses. They stood under a street lamp whose bulb Suresh had smashed with a stone. Though I couldn't understand why he had bothered to do that because all he and Meena did was talk to each other and sometimes, very rarely, hold hands. Of course, they didn't know I was watching them and didn't know that I'd seen a street dog peeing at the bottom of that street lamp earlier that evening and that sometimes, on the days they didn't manage to slip out of their houses, an old man leant his bicycle against the lamp and unzipped his trousers to the servant girls walking home with colourful plastic baskets.

But my parents still insisted on taking me with them when they went out. 'Three people can't go anywhere on a scooter,' I would argue.

'Of course they can't,' my father would reply. 'We are going by auto, and you are coming with us.'

So we rattled and bumped to a restaurant, cinema or shopping complex, Amma and Daddy on either side of me while I looked at the pictures and slogans the driver had painted on the inside of his vehicle – a picture of Dr Rajkumar and Swami Raghavendra, a lotus with 'Mother is Supreme God' written below it. 'Don't Kiss Me,' said the back of the lorry hurtling ahead of us, and 'We Two Our Two.'

There was almost no sound of traffic in Thiruninravur.

*   *   *

Janaki asked Sundar permission to visit the temple one morning just before he left for the office.

Amma had told me that the Sri Ranganathaswamy temple in Thiruninravur was supposed to look like the temple at Srirangam and to be nearly 200 years old, though no one really knew for sure. She had also told me about the intricate carving on its walls and about how powerful Sri Ranganatha, Vishnu sleeping on the ocean, was.

'Don't say you don't want to visit the temple if Sundar or Janaki ever decide to go,' she'd added.

'Yes, today would be a nice day to go,' Sundar said. 'It's a little less hot than usual.'

'Can I take Nithya and Sudha with me?' Janaki asked.

Sundar glanced at Sudha, who was standing at the kitchen door polishing a vessel with the end of her sari.

'All right,' he said. 'Only be careful not to lose each other. The temple is very crowded sometimes.'

As he wheeled his scooter out he asked Janaki how they meant to go.

'By bus – as usual.'

'Don't go by bus today. Take an auto-rickshaw.' And he gave her a twenty-rupee note, then rode away before she could say anything. I thought she looked surprised.

It had been a long time since I wore a pavadai. The silk swished and rustled around my ankles and the stone flags of the temple floor were cool and damp beneath my feet. Sudha did not own a silk sari but looked lovely this evening in her nylon one. She loved little outings like this, she'd told me as she had washed the turmeric paste off her face that afternoon. If only Janaki could go out more often. Janaki walked a little ahead of the two of us. She did not look up at the yakshis or apsaras or musical instruments or soot and sticky lamp oil on the walls and pillars. The temple smelt of flowers, camphor and jaggery and the sharp, tangy scent of tamarind paste being cooked with spices.

'Doesn't this make you feel hungry?' Sudha whispered to me.

When we stopped at the Ganesha shrine Janaki gave us each twenty-five paise to drop into the copper plate. The flame in the middle of the plate made my coin look like a gold one for a minute.

'*O Vakrathunda, Mahakaya, Surya koti* . . . God of the Curved Tusk and Mighty Body . . . remove all obstacles from my path,' the priest chanted.

'Fatty-fatty bombalatty,' a little boy chirruped from behind. He was sitting on the floor with the lamplight dancing in his eyes. Everyone turned to look at him. Only one or two people were smiling.

'Shut up!' his mother hissed, and put her hand over his mouth. 'You can't say that about God.' But Ganesha smiled back at the boy, kind and content with his trunk resting on his happy middle-aged-man's stomach, his four dimpled hands spread out in blessing. As we were coming in I had seen a couple breaking twenty-five coconuts to Ganesha outside the temple. The water had trickled stickily down the street, and the urchins had crouched around ready to leap at the white coconut pieces that bounced high off

70

the ground. The man had been panting when he'd finished, but when he had turned to his wife and dabbed his face with a piece of cloth, they had both smiled. They had paid off another debt.

Vishnu shone in his high-roofed shrine of black stone, lamps glowing around and above him as he lay fully stretched out on his enormous waterbed with the shadows of small reptiles' heads on his face, long lashes against his cheeks and the smile on his face soft and dreamy. I felt the waves swell and fall beneath him.

'Let this summer pass quickly,' I prayed. I couldn't think of anything else I really wanted.

I looked to see if Janaki and Sudha were praying. Sudha had her eyes squeezed shut like an obedient child, her lips solemnly moving. Her face was untroubled. The copper light played on Janaki's cheeks and mouth. *Kandarpa-darpa-hara sundara divya murthe* – Vishnu just might open his eyes, unwind his giant blue limbs and leap lightly over the iron barricades, looking at Janaki with a playfulness that never came into other eyes that looked at her. Maybe he would run his hands over her warm shoulders and arms, hidden beneath her pale cotton sari. And she would be one of those cowherd girls who left their husbands sleeping dully on sour pillows every night.

Minakrite kamatha kala narasimha varmain – he whirled and danced around us as we circled the temple. A slimy fish, a jewel-shelled turtle, a fiery old lion-face. At every little shrine Sudha dropped a coin from the little bundle at her waist and placed her hand over the hot camphor flames. She let the fire get too close to her palm.

'Be careful, you might burn yourself,' I whispered.

Janaki wasn't listening to either of us. An unkempt warrior, a little man, a prince, a baby who opened his mouth and showed that the universe spun between his sharp milk-teeth and his pink tongue.

The tip of Hari-the-temple-elephant's trunk felt velvety on the top of my head, like some old cloth-toy. 'Hurrrrump!' he blew gently at a little girl, who squealed and buried her face in her mother's sari. Hari's sides were a huge, wrinkled grey wall and his backside was as fat and shapely as that of a filmi village girl's. The pockmarked man who looked after him was proudly telling whoever would listen that Hari ate so many kilos of grass and hay, so many sticks of sugarcane, so much jaggery and so many bunches of bananas a day.

Once or twice every year Sri Ranganatha was hoisted on Hari's back and the musicians, priests and devotees chirped and hopped at his feet as they went in procession through the city. Many years later I was told that one day, a very long time after that visit to the temple with Janaki and Sudha, Hari, in a fit of unprophesied elephant-rage, picked up a worshipper and smashed him against the 200-year-old walls.

The old widows outside at the gate argued over which of them Janaki had left our three pairs of slippers with. Sudha cajoled them into dividing the money among them. They reluctantly agreed and watched Janaki with sad wet eyes as she untied her small cloth purse. We walked past the rows of vendors squatting on the pavements with copies of Andal's Thiruppavai, the Vishnusahasranama in Tamil, bangles, grinding stones, betel leaves and heaps and heaps of pink, yellow, red and white sugar sweets. I could see that Sudha wanted to linger but Janaki walked swiftly ahead.

Sundar had given us enough money to go back by auto-rickshaw as well, but it took us a while to find one. Sudha got in first, and then I did. As Janaki was climbing in someone stretched out an arm to her shoulder but didn't quite touch her. I peered out to see a woman standing by the auto, her hands spread out before us, the fingers decayed by leprosy into little brown stumps. The redness in her eyes could have been due to her disease but her breath smelt distinctly of toddy. Janaki stared at her helplessly. Between the three of us we only had a five- and a two-rupee note left, just enough to pay the driver when we got home.

The woman stepped back as the driver started his ancient engine with a bang and a burst of smoke. She suddenly thrust her big face at us, with a hole where her nostrils should have been, cursed and then laughed. The three of us drew back and the auto accelerated. But it was as if her drunken laughter, more real than her decaying body, had run behind us and leapt in through the rickshaw's open sides, demanding a place to sit.

*   *   *

Kodai came in with a message from her mother early one morning, when Janaki was still eating. Her parents wanted to go for an upanayanam that morning at Arani. They wanted to take Kodai with them, and Sridhar had to go to college. So could Janaki come and sit with Ambuja Pati?

73

'Tell your mother I will come.' Janaki was bent over her leaf so I couldn't see her face.

'Are you sure you can go?' Sudha asked. 'I can go if you want.'

'I will go,' Janaki repeated, and looked up at Kodai. 'Why don't you stay and eat something?'

Kodai hesitated for a minute, looking at the vessels of food spread out on the kitchen floor.

'No, I should go or they will be angry,' she said reluctantly. 'And anyway there will be lunch at the upanayanam.'

Janaki went after she had finished lunch. Sudha went up to her room. When she came down I saw that she had combed and re-plaited her hair.

'What are you doing?' she asked me.

'Practising percentage problems. I have to finish this set of sums by afternoon.'

Sudha didn't ask me any questions, as she sometimes liked to do when she saw me studying. Instead, she flung open the four windows of the front room and the two kitchen windows that looked into the backyard. Light streamed into the house in sloping conveyor belts of dancing dust. When Sundar came down the unexpected brightness made him blink. He sat on the floor and began reading his newspaper. Sudha flitted in and out busy with her usual morning chores, and I watched Sundar watch her from behind the *Hindu* – Sudha's just-visible ankles, Sudha's waist, back and neck, the clear, smooth, untouched skin of her cheeks and forehead. Like that other day when he had stood behind me and watched Sudha in the cowshed, he seemed puzzled.

He didn't move for a long time and I began to think

he'd fallen asleep when he asked her, 'How are your parents nowadays?' He never spoke to her when Janaki was around.

'They are well,' she replied.

'And is your brother doing well at school?'

'Oh, yes. He will sit for his SSLC exams in two years.'

'Good.' And he looked like he didn't know what else to say.

I couldn't concentrate on my work. Maybe I should take my books and go upstairs, I thought. But I didn't. Though Sundar stayed where he was in his chair and Sudha sat down next to me and began cleaning a tray of rice, they didn't say much to each other after that. A cuckoo sang from somewhere far away and another cuckoo replied from our garden or Kodai's. The red and green glass bangles Sudha wore tinkled and the house felt young and hopeful and content. Vasu, Kamala and Kodai would be at the upanayanam by now, which would smell of fire and ghee, and Kodai would eat too much.

I might have fallen asleep if Janaki hadn't returned. Sundar went upstairs again and Sudha shut the windows while Janaki was washing herself at the pump. I tried not to think about how different, how full of light the house had been without Janaki.

Two days after that Sundar decided to go to Madras for his cousin's daughter's wedding. He would be away for three days, he told us.

'I've bought enough vegetables for a week. There will be no need for anyone to go out while I'm away,' he said. So the front door was never opened, and the blue scooter which smelt of grease and the outdoors clumsily blocked the hallway. Janaki stayed up in her room nearly all the time and Sudha went about her work looking different, more lost and dreamy. Both of them were beginning to irritate me.

Because there was so little to do and think about, I opened the kitchen door one morning when I saw Kodai in Janaki's backyard.

'I haven't seen you for a long time,' she told me. 'I was beginning to think you had gone back to Bangalore.'

'How can I go back to Bangalore? There is no one there now,' I said impatiently.

Kodai shrugged. 'I just thought,' she said.

'I have been here all this while – in there.' I pointed to the house.

Kodai looked in the direction of my finger and her eyes narrowed with curiosity. I began to feel bored. It might have been better to have stayed inside after all.

'So you didn't talk to Raghu that day,' Kodai said.

'No, I didn't.'

I waited for her to say something more. She was drawing circles in the mud with a stick – surprisingly neat circles, little ones intertwined in dizzy patterns.

Kodai looked up. 'I have two dolls,' she said.

'You are too grown up to play with dolls,' I said scornfully. 'I gave away my dolls a long time ago.'

Mona Lisa with the bright golden hair, Pretty with the little mouth and Russian peasant dress – I still remembered them both well. Both of them sent from somewhere abroad by my father's friends. And the two smaller monkey-faced ones, bought unexpectedly when Amma and I were taking shelter from a downpour near a toy shop. I wondered where they had all gone to, and still recalled the pang I had felt when I

76

found one of their heads being used as a cricket ball by one of the neighbour's boys.

'I don't play with dolls any more,' I firmly repeated.

'Well, one of mine is a boy. A boy doll – have you ever had a boy doll?' Kodai asked.

I had to admit that I hadn't. I had never wanted a boy doll anyway.

'But it's more fun. There is much more you can do if you have two dolls, a boy and a girl,' Kodai said.

I looked at her thoughtfully. Fat, greedy and very stupid at school but also mysteriously grown up. Some of the girls at school clustered together in small, curious groups that giggled and whispered, groups I kept away from because I preferred to find things out for myself. I wondered how much Kodai already knew about – things?

'Shall I get my dolls?' she had stood up and asked eagerly. 'Let's play with them together. It will be a lot of fun.'

I imagined two naked pink plastic bodies with their absurd little clothes heaped in small untidy piles on the grass in Sundar's garden. 'We are too big to play with dolls,' I said resolutely.

'I'll get them anyway. Once we start you'll see that it's a lot of fun.' She was just beginning to lumber off in the direction of her house when Sridhar jumped over the bushes and came towards us.

'What are you two doing together?' he asked. He seemed to be in a good mood, seemed actually very happy. He was wearing a T-shirt. It was the first time I had seen anyone wear a T-shirt here – most of the men wore neat, half-sleeved cotton shirts when they went out and stayed bare-chested or in undershirts at home.

Sridhar's T-shirt made him look taller and stringier than ever. 'I (heart) New York,' it announced against a background of yellow and black buildings and dark-blue sky. I wondered where he had got it.

I wondered if they could hear us up in the house. Why didn't Janaki open her windows, push aside her sari-curtains and look out, wondering whose voices were wafting up to her window? And why didn't Sudha appear near the back door, glad that it was no longer so quiet and wondering if it was all right for her to join us? But the house remained silent, nearly all its green windows tightly shut. I saw Sridhar glance up once or twice towards what he probably thought was Sudha's room. I didn't tell him it did not overlook that part of the garden.

But he was determined to be in a good mood anyway. 'Come on, both of you. Let's go to the tamarind grove,' he said.

He meant the half acre of tamarind trees at the far end of the crude lane running behind the house. I already knew the grove was supposed to be haunted. We slipped over the bushes behind which Raghu had hidden some weeks ago. There were no houses here, and after the shade of Sundar's garden the sun beat down. It was nearly a ten-minute walk and Kodai was panting in five minutes. She squatted down in the middle of the lane and spat, a neat, round, white-bubbled pool.

'If you wait, you'll see that it evaporates in a few minutes,' she told me.

I turned away. 'I'm not waiting,' I said.

Sridhar hauled her up by the shoulder. 'It's hot out here. Let's get to the trees as fast as we can.'

He could walk very quickly. Kodai and I didn't even try to keep pace with him. He had tried to tuck in his shirt but it hung clumsily out of the waistband of his trousers as he galloped through the afternoon like some big awkward insect.

The grove was dark and cool but it didn't feel as if there were any ghosts in it. The trees were very old, with stiff peeling bark and surprisingly tiny leaves that drooped limply in the heat. Kodai began looking for tamarind pods but the ones scattered on the ground were green and raw. Sridhar reached up and plucked some of the riper ones that hung from the tips of the lower branches.

'You too take some,' Kodai invited me, and I broke open the fragile brown pods gingerly. Of course, I had eaten tamarind before but even these ripe ones were more sour than anything I had tasted before. I felt my mouth run dry and the hair on my face and back of my neck stand on end.

'Nithya has seen a ghost,' Sridhar said, laughing.

A long, cool, unexpected breeze floated through the trees and ruffled our hair. Sridhar's hair needed cutting. It lay flat on his forehead in a ridiculous fringe and nearly covered his eyebrows. Every now and then he would push it back with an impatient jerk of his neck.

'Many people died here during a famine in this district a hundred years ago,' he began telling us, 'and their ghosts would knock at the doors of rich people after dark, asking for food and water.'

I could imagine them – ghosts with hollow cheeks, concave stomachs and bony arms slobbering at windows, at the smells of boiling rice and roasted spices.

'And of course there are a whole lot of other ghosts as well,' Sridhar said. 'They all come here finally – to this grove, all the ghosts of the town.'

I didn't believe in ghosts.

'But where are they? Why haven't we seen any yet?' I asked, and two figures untwined themselves from behind a tamarind tree. The boy – he was probably not more than twenty years old – was wearing nothing but a lungi, which he tightened around his waist as he ran. The woman was older than he was, she was nearly as old as Janaki, and she found it more difficult to run quickly. Her sari ended just below her thick calves and she did not wear a blouse. We could see the dark-brown plumpness of her back and arms and shoulders. Her hair had come loose and she pushed it off her face as she ran. Sridhar, Kodai and I watched them and when they reached the edge of the grove the young man looked back at us and laughed, his beautiful white teeth flashing from between his dark lips. The woman kept her face turned away and refused to take the boy's hand when he offered it to her.

'Did we disturb them?' Kodai asked. No one answered her. 'What do you think they were doing here?' she turned to her brother, her voice high and childish. I could see her eyes glistening. She tugged at Sridhar's arm. 'What were they doing here? Did they come to pick tamarind?' she asked.

'I don't know. How am I to know why some idiot chooses to spend his afternoon under the trees when he should have been out working?' Sridhar asked. He sounded upset. He walked away from us further into the grove. Kodai opened her mouth to say something and then shut it again.

'Are you two coming with me? Or are you going back home?' Sridhar asked without looking back. Kodai ran up to him but I stayed where I was and wondered why I had agreed to come out with them in the first place.

'I want to go home. I'm sick of both of you,' is what I would have liked to have said, but I stayed on. My real home was far, far away, and there was nothing to do yet in Sundar's house. So I followed Sridhar and Kodai, though I made sure that I walked a little behind them and stopped to linger beneath every other tree.

'Look,' Kodai said, coming up to me and digging her elbow into my side. Iron nails had been driven into some of the tamarind tree trunks. I had never seen such big nails before. They were starting to rust.

'What would anyone want to do that for?' I asked.

'The ghosts live in these trees. People drive nails into the trunks to contain them – to make sure they don't get out,' Sridhar said softly.

I stared at him curiously. Did he really believe what he was telling us? And did the Jesuit fathers in his college even let them talk about these things? A horn blared somewhere outside the grove. Then it stopped and it was again very still. I suddenly realized there were no birds here, not even crows and sparrows.

And then Sridhar picked up a stone and knocked out one nail and then another and yet another. They were wedged deep inside the wood, so he was soon sweating and his palms had turned red.

'I've released the ghosts!' he called out. He laughed loudly, hysterically. The sound of his mirth whirred around our heads and slammed against the trees. Kodai screamed and ran blindly through the grove, hitting her forehead against a tree, followed by a hundred grinning dead men gesticulating madly.

I followed her, but I walked more slowly and looked back to see what Sridhar was doing. He had stopped laughing and was leaning against one of the trees, exhausted. There were little holes in the trunk where the nails had been. These and its outstretched limbs made it as tragic and grand as a man being crucified.

*   *   *

When I got back to Sundar's I told Sudha about our trip to the tamarind grove, though I left out the two people who'd run from behind the trees. But even as I talked I knew that Sudha wasn't listening. She sat in her room, her box of glass bangles open before her. Twelve red, eight yellow flecked with gold, and five deep-blue.

'I really shouldn't break so many,' she sighed, half to herself.

'So you, too, don't believe in ghosts?' I asked.

'Yes . . . oh, I don't know, Nithya! Why do you sometimes ask me these strange questions?'

I turned and walked to the door. Sudha had turned boring and stupid and was no fun to be with any more.

'I won't bother you again,' I shot over my shoulder.

She was at my side in an instant. 'Come on,' she said, putting her arm around my shoulders. '*Come on . . .* you can ask me anything you like,' she coaxed when I refused to look up. The three blue and green bangles on her wrist made deep undersea shadows on my white shirt. I went to sit on her mat.

She smiled at me gratefully and went to examine her face in the mirror. 'Pimples,' she sighed, and pointed to two of them on her forehead. 'My amma used to make a paste of something for my sister when she had pimples.'

'If you have pimples you have pimples – and that's it,' I said in exasperation. I wondered if all twenty-year-olds talked like this. Sudha was still looking at herself, her eyes half shut, her eyelashes thick as a pretty child's. When she reached up and pushed her hair off her face I remembered that the woman in the tamarind grove had done the same thing.

'Pimples – and no long hair,' Sudha said, and wrinkled her nose in comic despair.

When she came down later to cook dinner, the three bangles and the nose ring shone as brightly as ever and her face was dusted lightly with talcum powder. Janaki came down only when she heard Sundar's knock. I had forgotten that he was to return that evening from Madras. Janaki opened the door for him and he went directly to the backyard for a bath. Sudha, who had been sitting by the stove, turned around and looked up at him but he didn't seem to notice her, nor did he talk to Janaki during dinner. He went upstairs after his meal and I watched Sudha bend low over the stove scrubbing it fiercely. Her bangles tinkled against it, and when one of them broke she removed the other two. Janaki came and stood at the kitchen door and I saw that she was looking at Sudha.

'Go up to your room. I'll finish cleaning the kitchen,' she said. Sudha went upstairs without a word.

Janaki's eyes were thoughtful as she swept the kitchen and put away the vessels. She didn't talk to me. Sudha had left her bangles behind on the

83

floor. Janaki picked them up and looked at them for a minute before placing them on a shelf.

When I came down the next morning Sundar and Sudha were alone in the kitchen. Janaki must have been in the garden. Sudha was telling Sundar something I couldn't quite hear and laughing up at him. Because he had his back to me I couldn't see if he was smiling back. But when he spoke to Sudha his voice was as it always was – steady, low and unexcited. She smiled at him and handed him a tumbler of coffee. Sundar took it from her and reached out to touch the tip of her ear with the other hand as if she were a soft little animal.

I wondered if I should go into the kitchen and startle them. I decided to wait behind the door a little longer, half hidden by the shadows. The back door was pushed open just then and Janaki came in, her hair tied in a white towel. She'd probably washed it earlier that morning. I couldn't guess if she too had seen what Sundar did or if she thought it strange that Sundar and Sudha were standing so close to each other. She walked straight into the front room, a little dazed after the brightness outside. She saw me, gave a little start and then looked at me curiously. Maybe she wondered what I was doing there, behind the kitchen door, but she didn't ask me any questions – Janaki never, ever did. She just went upstairs.

Chapter Four

I soon got the feeling that Sudha began to like being by herself. She went about her work humming songs I didn't know and stayed in her room whenever she could. But she was also restless sometimes. She would then come looking for me and want to talk. I could sense excitement in her, and fear, and something else I didn't have a name for.

It was her idea that we both go out to buy oil at Kumar Oil Depot. Sundar normally brought home the month's supply of oil and soap and everything else for the house, but he was getting forgetful. When Janaki discovered one morning that there was just enough oil for one more meal, he had already left for work.

'Let me go and get it,' Sudha offered. 'I know where to go.'

'You will go alone?' Janaki asked.

'Can I take Nithya with me?'

Janaki frowned. 'I don't know if you two should go by yourselves.'

'Please,' Sudha pleaded. I didn't say anything.

Janaki looked at her curiously. 'Go, then, if you want to,' she said, and handed us the money. She went off to her room as if the question had nothing to do with her now.

I didn't know whether Sudha had offered to get the oil because she wanted to please Sundar, to spare him the trouble of going out again just after he got back home, or simply because she wanted to get out of the house. She used to tell me about going to village fairs with her sisters, counting and recounting the money they had saved up.

'I don't know why you want to go,' I told her. 'And why did you have to drag *me* out as well?'

'Why?' she looked surprised. 'I thought you'd *want* to come.'

I hadn't been out of the house since my trip to the haunted trees with Sridhar and Kodai, but I had still hoped to stay indoors that day. The sun blazed down on us and the light hurt my eyes. The oil store was about seven miles from the house. There were many stores much closer, newer and cleaner ones, but we all knew that my grandfather and his father had always patronized this one.

'The oil is unadulterated,' Sundar would say if someone asked him if it was really necessary to go all the way to Kumar's shop. 'Not like the rubbish you get here.'

Sudha and I would have to catch a bus to get there. The bus went all the way to the district headquarters at Arani but also made several stops in Thiruninravur. As we walked down the road, Seshadri passed us. I had never noticed how bald he was, how the few strands on the back of his head were kept very long and carefully combed sideways and upwards to cover as much of his scalp as possible. It looked like an oily, clumsily woven mat.

'It will rain later today,' he stopped to tell us. He had stopped at Sundar's gate once or twice before when I had been outside, and shared his weather forecast for the day.

'What makes him think he knows?' I whispered to Sudha. I didn't care if he was within earshot. 'What does he think he is – God?'

Sudha smiled but said, 'Let him be. It doesn't harm anyone, does it? And anyway I think he actually knows quite a bit.'

I still preferred to be bad-tempered and disagreeable that day.

Seshadri had been carrying an umbrella against the sun. Sudha had forgotten ours. 'Do you think he's worried about his complexion?' she said, turning to me and smiling. She was trying to cheer me up.

We had to wait nearly forty minutes for the bus. 'How much longer, Sudha?' I whined every now and then, knowing that she had no idea. The bus finally lumbered up in a cloud of diesel fume and dust. It was crowded and we had to squeeze ourselves into a thicket of strange smells and sweaty underarms. It seemed a long time since I had been in a bus. The morning might be an exciting one after all.

Sudha scrambled in her cloth purse for coins. 'We should give him the exact fare or we'll never get our change back,' she said firmly. The conductor took the money and continued pushing his way through the crowd.

'What about my tickets?' Sudha asked.

Someone prodded her on the back. 'Why do you want to bother him for tickets? You're getting off at Government School Stop, aren't you?'

Sudha turned to me. 'The cheat!' she whispered fiercely. I smiled at her indignation. They did this all the time in Bangalore.

Though we never discussed it even after we finally got home that evening, I've often wondered how we missed our stop. The conductor shouted out the names of every point the bus drew up at. But he was probably annoyed by Sudha's reaction to his taking the money without issuing tickets, or maybe he had even overheard her calling him a cheat. And the other passengers had been too involved in a quarrel over the space a sack of rice was taking up to notice that we'd missed our stop.

'This is the last stop before we head for Arani,' the conductor said, yawning leisurely. Suddenly we realized that we had been on the bus for a long while. Sudha had been telling me about her two trips from her village to Thiruninravur.

'Hey, you! Do you want to go to Arani? Yes, you do look like the type who has an important government job!' the conductor called out sarcastically.

'We've missed our stop!' she exclaimed, and we elbowed a passage to the door. A few damp hands obligingly pushed us through. I stumbled out onto the road, blinking in the light.

'Where are we?' I asked.

'I don't know. But we can't be that far away from where we need to go.'

I agreed. 'Yes, nothing can be too far away from anything else here. This is the smallest town in the world.'

'Is it?' Sudha said doubtfully.

'Of course it is.'

We had begun to feel wild and adventurous. We didn't care which direction we walked in, kicking up small clouds of dust and hearing the two oil vessels clink against each other in the bag Sudha carried.

'Let's not ask anyone the way right now,' I suggested.

'Yes, let's not,' she agreed, just a little hesitantly.

The lanes were even narrower than in our part of town, and much more crowded. On GC Street the houses were fairly large. Surrounded by their own gardens and walled in by bushes and trees, they spread themselves out sleepily in the sun. The houses here were interspersed with shops, built close together, running into each other like restless little brown lizards. A few men turned and looked at Sudha. She seemed oblivious to the attention she was attracting. When I said, 'Walk on this side,' and placed myself between her and the world, she wanted to know why. I wondered at how stupid she could be at times.

A statue of MG Ramachandran, chief minister and big, sky-blazing film star, stood at the end of the lane where we had got off. The orange flowers around his neck were still fresh. I wondered who clambered up there and garlanded the statue every day, and whether the plastic sunglasses perched precariously on that famous nose ever fell off or cracked or got bleached transparent by the sun. A narrow crooked lane lined with huts tilting against each other branched off from the lane. Film music blared out of the two speakers tied to MGR's feet – *Naan aanayital . . . adha nadanthuvitaal . . .*

'I love that song.' Sudha's eyes sparkled. 'I've even seen the film.'

But I knew she wasn't really an MGR fan. He belonged to a generation before hers. Like all good Tamil brahmin girls, she looked upon Kamalhasan – a slim, fair, true-blooded Iyengar – as her special hero.

Two old men squatted below the statue. I thought they were beggars and was wondering whether I should ask Sudha for a coin to give them, when I saw that they were selling packets of rubber bands that were so old and discoloured they might already have been used. One of the men noticed me staring and nodded encouragingly. When he smiled his mouth was so red with betel juice that I thought he was bleeding.

'Come on – what are you looking at?' Sudha tugged at my arm.

'Where are we going now?'

'I don't know,' she said.

We walked up the road, then down, and up again past shops selling mounds of puffed rice, sacks of onion and garlic, trays of eggs, meat. Sudha hurried past a bakery displaying, in its fly-dotted glass counter, a single saffron, white and bilious-green cake, the circle of blue jam at its centre beginning to trail off drunkenly.

'I'm hungry,' I announced.

Sudha looked at me in horror. 'No, you can't be hungry!' she said. 'There is nothing for you to eat out here.'

'But I *am* hungry.'

The signboards on both little restaurants on this road said, 'Military Hotel'.

'Do you know what that means?' Sudha asked me.

'Of course I do.'

'And you still want to eat here?'

'I'm hungry,' I repeated obstinately.

So we stopped outside one of them. But when I went up to it I decided that I only wanted a cup of coffee.

'Why don't you go inside and take a seat?' the man at the counter asked, looking at us curiously.

'No, we'll wait here.' Sudha turned away and looked resolutely out into the street, trying not to smell the strange smells or think about the strange food inside.

I held my glass of coffee carefully. I had never seen coffee served in a *glass* glass before. I'd seen it in stainless steel cups, of course, and in porcelain mugs at Bangalore restaurants and sometimes at friends' houses. The coffee was stronger than anything I'd ever tasted and needed twice the amount of sugar I usually used. I wondered if anyone from our street ever came here. Sridhar, perhaps, or Sundar.

'What if we see Kodai's brother somewhere around here? Or someone else we know?' I asked Sudha after paying for the coffee with the money she gave me. 'Maybe even Sundar . . .' I looked carefully up at her.

She turned pale. Our adventure had begun to lose its charm for her.

'They wouldn't come to these parts of town,' she said, and began walking away.

I hurried after her. I didn't want to lose Sudha. It was the middle of the afternoon and even the two rubber-band vendors had moved away, finding the squat shadow of the MGR statue inadequate. The road was suddenly almost empty. A child began to cry inside one of the little houses. The door swung open and his mother, sweat-streaked and enormous with pregnancy, pushed him out into the street.

'Stay out there!' she screamed, and slapped him on the face.

He staggered back and cried out louder than before, long, high-pitched toneless cries. His eyes were dry and very wide-open.

'Let's get away from here,' Sudha begged. Her voice was shaking. I couldn't understand why she was so agitated. When we looked back, the woman had run out again and was grabbing the child to her, pressing its face against her swollen stomach.

For a moment I thought I had lost Sudha. She was walking fast, almost running down a crooked side street, passing blindly over torn pieces of newspaper, slogans scribbled in red, banana peels and a dead bird smashed shapelessly into the ground. I tried to catch up with her and for the first time realized how long and strong her legs were beneath the folds of the brown sari she was so fond of. She turned into an alley that branched off the one we entered and then into another before I caught up with her.

'Where do you think you are going?' I asked, grabbing her arm. We were both panting.

'What does it matter? We're lost anyway,' she said listlessly.

'And you have got us even more lost. How do you think we're going to get out of here?'

The houses around us were little more than huts, with low toy doors and grey thatched roofs that gaped open in sections. There were dozens of them. I had no idea so many people lived in Thiruninravur. Something was scribbled in charcoal again and again on one of the walls.

'What does that say?' I wanted to know. I had only begun learning to read Tamil when I first came here, and then only because it had given me something to do.

'*Hindi Ozhige,*' Sudha said without interest. *Get rid of Hindi.*

'I thought that happened twenty years ago.'

'I don't know. They haven't finished with it here.' Or maybe these graffiti were more than twenty years old. The sun and the occasional December gusts of cyclone rain made no difference to them.

I looked around me. Why was there no one in sight? The world was empty and still. Everyone had crawled into their houses away from the mid-afternoon sun. Or maybe there had been a riot or communal clash. This was something like how the markets in Bangalore looked in newspaper photographs when curfew had been declared – uneasy, haunted and silent. But this was Thiruninravur. There were no riots here, or revolutions. Only once in a long while, some stray wind picked up black and red slogans from Madras or Madurai or Trichi and slapped them onto these mud and plaster walls.

'Maybe we should go knock at one of those doors,' I suggested, 'and ask someone to help us get out of here.'

'I'm not going anywhere near them,' Sudha said obstinately.

'Why not?'

'Because I don't want to.'

I stared at her. 'All right, then, stay lost for ever.'

She didn't say anything to that. Her lips were dry

and tender on her face and a little bit of kajal was smudged in the corner of one of her eyes.

Ding-a-chik-a, ding-a-chik-a, ding-a-chik . . . That's how the drumbeats sounded as they came our way, very low at first and then louder and louder. Mournful and weepy sometimes, and then suddenly exuberantly festive. It looked like a funeral was coming our way. I had seen *their* funerals before, the stiff corpse wrapped in a white shroud carried high above everyone's heads, the wailing mourners beating their chests and the dancers before the procession. I also knew that although they were Hindus they didn't cremate their dead like we did; they buried them.

But it wasn't a funeral after all. It was a religious procession. Six men had the goddess, an amman, hoisted on their shoulders. Many of the men and women who followed carried trays of fruit and clay pots stuffed with flowers. That's why the alley had seemed so empty – almost everyone was out here. Men and boys twisted madly to the drumbeats. *Ding-a-chik-a* . . . They writhed around, leapt up in the air and flapped their hands in unexpectedly delicate movements.

Sudha and I were quickly swallowed by the procession. It felt a little like our bus ride – warm bodies and unfamiliar smells. But here everyone was moving around us, dancing, laughing or turning around to call to someone else over the music. The amman swayed against the blue sky. Her thick, coarse hair spread over her shoulders and down her back, her eyes were huge and angry and her cave of a mouth opened to reveal sharp teeth and a blood-stained tongue that would dart out to lick her plump, juicy lips any

94

minute. I wanted to know what they worshipped her for – against smallpox or madness, for rain, for money – for what? And where was she kept after the procession? In which little stone temple with doors always flung open, out of which she could wander into the sun and rain whenever she felt like it, her clothes and hair carelessly flying around her? The men groaned and sweated beneath her, their bones aching with the relentless stamp and thrust of her feet.

One little girl, very black-skinned with a thatch of dry brown hair, pushed her way to the front of the procession and began dancing with the men, her small limbs even more quick and agile than theirs. 'Oh, our ammu has become a boy!' someone shouted, and everyone laughed. But no mother or older sister grabbed her by the shoulder and dragged her back into the crowd.

I knew that most of the men and some of the women were drunk. I was half-nauseated, half-excited by the smells of palm toddy and garlic. I saw Sudha flinch and gasp for breath. I thought she would vomit here, in the middle of this crowd, on these feet coated with red dust. An old woman peered down at me curiously. Her face was dark and shrivelled, like a mango seed sucked dry. With the back of her hand she wiped off a gummy grey liquid that had gathered in the corner of one beady eye, set deep in her face.

'Who are you?' she asked me. 'I haven't seen you here before.'

A younger woman overheard her and peered over her shoulder. She was very drunk and her matted black, brown and red hair lay on her shoulder like rough coils of rope.

'Is that your sister?' the second woman asked, jerking her head at Sudha, who was clutching at my arm.

'Yes,' I nodded. 'My sister.'

'She is very beautiful,' the second woman said, and smiled at Sudha appreciatively,. She ran one unsteady finger down one side of her face. Sudha looked down at her stonily.

One of the men brought a large brown rooster with a very scarlet comb, swung him by his trussed legs before the goddess and set him down. The crowd surged forward to watch. I felt myself being carried forward. I was weightless and unimportant, a piece of driftwood. Another man, his forehead streaked with ash and vermilion, knelt before the rooster, untied its legs and made it stand upright. It staggered up on horny legs, dazed and uncertain of what was happening for the single second it took to slice its head off. The sharp knife made a neat shining arc through the air and blood spouted up in a little fountain, with one or two drops landing on the priest's cheek. He flicked them off gently with his fingertips and the drummers, who had stopped to watch, took up their beat again.

I looked at Sudha. She had screwed her eyes shut. I, too, wished I hadn't had to witness that. I'd never seeen an animal killed before. I hadn't thought there would be so much blood. I wondered what they would do with the rooster now. Cook him? Make children who were unhappy without any good reason, sick with mysterious ailments, drink his blood? I was worried that I would have to see him carried off with stiff limbs and rumpled feathers, a neat coin of red flesh where his head had been.

Someone pushed me aside, digging at my side so

sharply that I gasped for breath. 'Move aside, you fool,' someone else hissed. 'Can't you see what has happened?'

'What has happened?' I asked bewildered.

'I don't know,' Sudha said. 'I wish we could get out of this.'

But no one was listening to us. A sudden shriek pierced the crowd – from the woman who had just pushed past me. She was small and slight, different from the other women only in that she was very neatly dressed, her hair oiled and plaited. But when she reached the goddess, she cried out once more, her eyes rolling skywards.

'The goddess has come over her again,' someone near me exclaimed, and they watched her wide-eyed. She tore at her hair and swayed, her eyes burning like live coals. The drummers began to beat so loudly that I felt my ears buzz.

The people around us opened and closed and opened their big wet mouths and I didn't know whether they were singing or praying or talking to one another. The drummers writhed and leapt as if they too were possessed. Soon, though, everyone had stopped dancing. Only the possessed woman rocked and jerked like a clumsy doll, reaching for the goddess's feet with urgent hands.

In just a few minutes she fell down exhausted. I heard her moan once or twice, and then she lay quite still. The others gathered around her and touched her clothes and face gently, reverently. After she'd been lifted up and carried into one of the houses, the procession continued, but most of the crowd had broken away and gone indoors or moved into small groups, talking. The drummers too were beginning to tire, but the six men with the goddess bouncing on their shoulders trotted on.

Sudha and I were suddenly alone in the middle of the alley. No one paid any attention to us. She had turned pale and when she tried to walk, she stumbled. She might have fallen if I hadn't caught her arm.

'What's the matter?' I asked.

'It's so hot,' she muttered.

'It isn't all that bad,' I said firmly, though it was. 'And don't faint here. We don't know anybody who will help us.' I half dragged, half helped her into another lane. The houses, though still small, were no longer hovels.

'We've lost the vessels,' Sudha said suddenly, her voice rising hysterically. 'What will they say at home? Let me go and check . . .' She started to run back to the spot where the procession had stopped.

'You stay where you are,' I said. 'Let me go look for them.'

The vessels were still there in their bag. When I returned Sudha was sitting on the side of the road, her head buried in her knees but one hand held cautiously over the pouch at her waist where the money was. She looked up when I placed the vessels on the ground next to her with a clang.

'How are we going to get back home now?' I asked. The question hung heavy between us in the hot still afternoon. *How are we going to get back home?* I was increasingly tired and unbearably hungry. My head was throbbing and my eyes hurt whenever I raised them off the ground. But I knew I had to get the two of us home. Sudha was too tired and frightened.

'I don't understand why you are so upset,' I told her. She looked at me and smiled listlessly. I thought she was about to cry.

'I don't know what Sundar is going to say about all this,' I said very slowly and deliberately, without looking at Sudha or waiting for her reply.

'Get up and come along – if you want to.' I picked up the bag and began walking swiftly. I could hear the flap of her chappals behind me. It was simple – we only had to go back the way we had come and wait for the bus.

But we had got much further away from the main road than I had thought. The town had suddenly turned into a maze, with streets that twisted back onto themselves and bumped without warning into dead ends. We walked for a while and found ourselves back in the lane into which Sudha had first run. It must have been about 4 o'clock and was getting less hot. Maybe Seshadri Mama had been right about rain – when I looked up at the sky I saw a few grey clouds scuttle reluctantly across like difficult sheep, and felt a damp breeze against the back of my neck. Things might be more bearable if it started to rain now. I needed just to stand there for a few minutes and not think . . .

Someone was walking on the other side of the road. There were many people about now, but this was someone I recognized. Big head, oversized spectacles, a mouth so wide it might have been painted on.

'That's Raghu!' I said excitedly. And I noticed for the first time the awkwardness of his walk – bow-legged, head thrown backwards, a small hump just below his neck.

'Do you know him?' Sudha asked me, puzzled.

'Just a little bit. But who cares? He'll help us.' And I started to run across to him.

'How do you know he'll help us?' Sudha whispered sharply.

'He just will.'

I could see that he recognized me, though he hadn't expected me to come over to him. A sudden flicker of happiness leapt into his eyes.

'What does he think?' I thought scornfully. 'That Janaki has sent me to him?' But I smiled nicely. Sudha had come to stand by my side and was staring down at him, her eyes big with wonder, too confused to protest or ask questions.

'We think we're lost,' I said. 'We came out to buy oil and missed our bus stop,' I explained.

'Ask him if he'll help us get home,' Sudha whispered to me. She then turned to Raghu and asked him herself: 'Will you help us get home?'

He didn't say anything; he only nodded and walked on, signalling us to follow. It had begun to drizzle steadily now – I felt the sharp drops sting my face and saw them settle like silver beads on Raghu's and Sudha's hair. I sensed that we were going to a different part of town. Raghu stopped in front of a large house with a verandah. None of the houses on GC Street were as large as this one.

'This is where I live,' Raghu told us. It was the first time I had ever heard him say anything. His voice was unexpectedly deep – like a real man's, I thought in surprise. I peered at him through the rain to make certain it was really he who had spoken.

'Maybe you should take shelter here for a while,' he suggested.

'No . . . no.' Sudha sounded agitated. 'We don't mind getting wet. We're already very late.'

'It might be more sensible to wait here – just for a few minutes,' he said. 'The rain won't last much longer than that.'

'Let's wait,' I told Sudha, hoping to catch a glimpse of whoever else lived in this house. But although we stood there for nearly a quarter of an hour watching the warm, steady rain, we didn't hear the sound of voices or children crying or even the clink of vessels inside.

'That's how Sundar's house will sound if Sudha goes back to her village,' I thought.

Only once, a middle-aged woman looked out through the doorway, first at the rain and then at Sudha and me, calmly and without curiosity. I wondered who she was – Raghu's sister maybe, because Raghu couldn't be married. Kodai later told me that he lived all by himself except for two servants, and that his mother's people were supposed to have left him all that money. In a few minutes, a man came in with coffee for us. 'The glasses are actually made of silver,' Sudha whispered to me. I thought she would decline but she went right ahead and took one.

When the rain stopped as abruptly as it had started, Raghu fetched an auto-rickshaw. There was no real need for him to come back with us, but he stepped in, sitting as far from us as possible and not saying a word except to instruct the driver to stop at Kumar's. He got off to buy the oil himself, and only accepted the money Sudha offered when she said that too many questions would be asked if she returned it unspent.

Sudha tumbled out of the auto when it drew to a

stop a few yards from our gate. I got out more slowly and turned to look at Raghu, who was crouching back in the seat as if to make sure that no one who might be looking out of the house would see him. I knew that he probably wanted to look out of the auto himself and see someone's shadow outlined against a window. The auto had already wheeled around and chugged away when I realized we had forgotten to thank him.

It was six in the evening and already getting dark because of the rain. The houses loomed before us, bulky and shifting in the shadows. Janaki opened the door for us. I looked for Sundar's scooter behind her but it wasn't there. Even I was relieved to know that he hadn't returned.

'We got lost . . .' Sudha's voice was trembling. Janaki looked at the two of us as we stood at the door, dirty and damp.

'Go in and have your baths,' was all she said.

Chapter Five

I was walking up a hill. There was nothing green on it, only thorny bushes of no particular colour. My throat was as dry as the ground. But there were many small secret creatures with scales and flickering tongues behind the rocks and I needed to know about them. I had left school and my parents behind, at the bottom. But Sundar's house with its closed windows and softly shutting doors was still close by. Somewhere I would find a wall that I'd have to climb over to keep exploring. When I came to it, I discovered that it was much higher and harder to scale than I had thought. When I landed on the rough grass on the other side, it was with a shock that made me wake up and wonder where I was.

I looked across the room at Janaki, who seemed to be asleep. It was a full-moon night. I never could remember to keep track of the moon. Its light filtered in through the curtains. I thought I heard a sound outside the door and held my breath. But I must have imagined it. The house was as still as the square patch of sky outside the window.

It was dull lying there on the floor with a thin cotton sheet over me. I would go downstairs for a drink of water, I decided, though there was a jug in the corner of Janaki's room. It was darker than I had thought it would be as I crept down the stairs. My feet had to fumble for each step.

'Where has the moon gone?' I thought. But when I pushed open the kitchen window it was still there flooding the garden, though there was nothing to see outside. No Kodai seized by midnight hunger pangs come to gather gooseberries, no Sridhar lounging by the well or Raghu trying to squeeze through the bushes and creep as close to Janaki's house as he could.

I washed my glass and kept it carefully alongside the ones my grandmother had brought with her on her wedding day nearly forty years ago. When the sun rose and they all came downstairs, it was important that they not find out that I had been there at midnight.

Someone *was* moving about upstairs. I had to see who it was. I climbed up the stairs quickly. The doors of the two bigger bedrooms were shut, and the fat sacks of rice and tamarind leaned shapelessly against each other in the storeroom.

Sundar pushed open Sudha's door and shut it carefully behind him. I saw the flicker of a kerosene lamp for the instant the door was open: so Sudha wasn't asleep. Nor was Janaki. She was standing in the shadows near the rice and didn't seem to know that I was watching too. After she went back to her room, I waited for a while before following her. I slipped into bed but did not sleep for a while because I had to find out whether Janaki was asleep or lying awake, cold and still and waiting.

If she had noticed that I had been out of our room for some time that night, she didn't ask me any questions the next day. But then she hadn't asked me about what had happened to Sudha and me the day we had got lost, either. I had tried to find out whether Sundar had been told, but he didn't ask me anything though Sudha had looked upset the next morning. I asked her if Sundar had been angry with her the night before. She looked at me strangely.

'I didn't even see your Sundar Mama last night,' she said. 'It's just that I have a headache.'

She was beginning to complain of a headache far too often. And yet her eyes sometimes shone with a kind of . . . excitement that made her even more lovely than before.

*   *   *

I went in search of Kodai. Maybe she could tell me some of the things I now felt I needed to know, though of course I couldn't *ask* her about them. Sridhar was leaning on the gate staring across the road at nothing. He looked at me as if he didn't quite know me.

'Is your sister at home?' I asked. He didn't reply.

'Has Kodai gone out?' I asked, louder this time, as though I were talking to someone who was known to be going deaf.

'She hasn't got back from visiting Narayan Mama's daughter-in-law. She went with my mother.'

I turned away.

'Stay for a minute,' he said, 'and tell me how are things at home?'

105

What had he got to know – he and his fat, snooping sister? I stared at him suspiciously.

'What do you want to know?'

'I only asked how your Sundar and Janaki are,' he said. 'And Sudha.'

'Oh, them. They're all right.'

'I heard that you and Sudha wandered into the slums the other day.'

'Who told you that?'

'People saw you, of course!' He sounded surprised. 'I go there myself – often,' he added in a low voice.

'Really?'

'Yes. And anyway this is not Madras or Bangalore, you know. We get to know about things – somehow.'

And I hated this prying little town which would soon find out *things* that only I still knew about, grab my secrets and scatter them into the air in chattering handfuls.

'So Raghu has been talking to you?' I asked.

'What has Raghu got to do with it?' He seemed genuinely puzzled.

'Nothing,' I said quickly. I should have known that Raghu wouldn't say anything.

'Raghu seems to like your family,' Sridhar said, leaning towards me and smirking. 'That's one thing most people haven't found out yet.'

This was irritating. I didn't want to hear what Kodai had told me about Raghu and Janaki all over again, even if Sridhar had something new to add. I wanted to know whether Janaki or even Sundar knew about whatever Raghu felt for Janaki. Probably not.

'But Raghu doesn't like your uncle,' Sridhar whispered. 'He thinks Sundar is cruel to Janaki.'

Cruel? That startled me. 'How do you know that?' I asked.

'How do I know that?! Because Raghu is quite a good friend of mine, that's why I know that,' he said. 'One of the few men who *thinks*, in this hole we live in. And then only because he got away from – this place.' He waved his hand up and down GC Street gloomily. 'I don't know why *I* continue to live here.'

I wanted to ask him where else he thought he could go, but there were other, more important things I needed to know.

'Why does Raghu think Sundar is – mean to Janaki?'

'Oh, I'm not sure. Raghu keeps to himself, you know. He only talks to me once in a while, when everything gets too much for him. He says it's because of Sundar that Janaki is shut up in that house all the time.'

I remembered what Amma had once told me. 'But even my amma once said there is nothing left for Janaki to do,' I told Sridhar. 'She's a widow.'

'I tried telling Raghu that that's the way most people think – not me, of course. But Raghu doesn't think that way. I think he'd even marry her if Sundar would let him.' He grinned.

'What makes him think *Janaki* would want to marry him?' I didn't know why the thought made me so angry.

'Yes, she'd object to his mother not being one of us, wouldn't she? I think he knows that. They don't let you forget such things out here.'

'It's not that. He's – he's not *normal*!' I said.

'Yes, that could be seen as a problem,' Sridhar agreed. 'But why are you getting so upset about it? We all know, and Raghu too knows, there is no reason to believe that anything will change . . . for Janaki.'

'I'm not upset about anything.'

'All right, you're not,' he smiled. 'But tell me – why does Sundar not get married?'

I was beginning to think Sridhar was an even bigger gossip than his mother. 'How am I to know all that?' I said. 'You've forgotten – I am here only for six months.'

'Do you think he gets what he wants anyway? That's why he doesn't care to marry?' Sridhar had lowered his voice.

'What do you mean?'

He smiled and didn't say anything.

Tell me – tell me what do you mean by that? How much do you know? I was filling with a panic I could not explain.

'I asked you something,' I reminded him quietly, and watched with disgust as he lowered and raised one bulging eyelid in a ghastly slow motion of a wink.

'More men than we can guess visit . . . prostitutes. I wonder if anyone I know does . . .' He looked at me. 'Do you know about prostitutes?'

I nodded because I did know. More or less.

*　　*　　*

I decided to explore Sundar's room that afternoon. I had to wait for a while because Sudha had decided to feed and milk Lakshmi earlier than usual and was taking a long while over it. I heard her cooing to the buffalo as if it were a baby. I found the gentleness of her voice and her slow, luxurious movements exasperating. I wanted her to hurry up. But even after she had finished and gone up to her room Janaki didn't sleep for a while. When I went in I saw that she had pushed aside the curtain and was sitting on my mattress, looking out the window.

'Do you want to lie down?' she asked when she saw me standing near the door.

'No, I'll stay downstairs.' And after a while I sneaked up the stairs and peered in quietly to see if she was asleep.

It was nearly four in the afternoon when I went into Sundar's room. My heart thumped, even though I didn't know what I was looking for. I had never been in there alone or for very long before and it would be exciting to feel the unfamiliar furniture, to thrust my hands into corners and crevices I hadn't visited.

The late-afternoon sun slanted in through the windows and I felt a pang of disappointment because the room felt clean, sparse and unmysterious. I walked around the bed – the only bed in the house, because everyone else slept on the floor. The chest of drawers that stood against one wall seemed very old, and though it was unpolished and stained I sensed it was made of very good wood. I tapped it with my knuckles as I had seen my father do in furniture and timber shops. The sound was loud in the silence. What if Janaki or Sudha thought it was someone knocking at the front door and came out to answer it and found me in here? I froze where I stood, ready to dash below the bed if I heard footsteps. The thought of being found out sneaking around Sundar's room was terrifying. But the house remained silent. I tiptoed to the door and shut it before I continued exploring.

I opened a drawer and saw a small bundle of rupee notes and a file. I pulled the file out and opened it to look at the papers inside. Marks cards with N.

Sundararajan's name on them. SSLC, Standard 12, B. Com. An appointment letter. Photocopies of land and house papers and bank statements, some with Janaki's name on them. I tried to make sense of them but had to give up. There were no photographs to look at or old letters to read.

The second drawer was even more unexciting. A strip of Avil, two strips of Digene, a bottle of liquid Gelusil and another of Eno Fruit Salts. I hadn't known that Sundar suffered from indigestion, that he belched and sourly burped when the rest of us couldn't hear. Some shiny, new iron nails wrapped in a piece of newspaper, a pair of blunt scissors, Scotch tape, a brightly coloured picture of a butter-smeared Krishna, two ink pens, a bottle of grey-black Bril ink, and an empty notebook with a musty smell. The lowest drawer was locked. I jerked at the handle, but it wouldn't open.

I lay down on the bed. The pillow and mattress were firmer and less lumpy than any other in the house, and the sheets were cool. I wondered if Sudha ever came in here, and felt a strange excitement run down my legs. I jumped up impatiently and groped beneath the mattress. I held my breath – I could feel something. It must be something secret or Sundar wouldn't have bothered to hide it. It was a small packet of Charminar cigarettes. I sniffed hard, loving the smell of slightly stale tobacco. There was also a small packet labelled Nirodh. I didn't bother to open it. Some kind of medicine, perhaps, or Band-Aid that he'd thrust there absent-mindedly and forgotten.

*   *   *

Because I shared Janaki's room, I sensed something cold and resentful growing inside her and settling in the pit of her stomach in hard, tight coils. She hardly ever spoke to Sudha, and I also noticed that she made it a point to serve Sundar every meal and stay in the kitchen till he had gone upstairs. I woke up one or two nights to find her sitting up on her bed, her sheet drawn around her.

'What is she waiting for?' I wondered. For a door to open, for the soft sounds of careful footsteps and the creak and click of another door? Would she burst out of her own room one night and cry out, flinging whatever she was feeling at their startled faces? I didn't fully understand what it was. Bitterness or loneliness or a hunger that she had been told to forget but that insisted on rearing up its lizard head every once in a while and that now, provoked by Sudha's youth and loveliness, was beginning to gnaw at her with small, sharp teeth? She didn't ever leave the house – she haunted it like a small, pale ghost – except once, when she wanted to go to the Sri Ranganathaswamy Temple.

'I don't think you should go by yourself,' Sundar said. 'Why don't you take Nithya?' His voice was gentle, as though he were talking to a child he felt he should remember to be nice to more often.

'I don't think I want to go today, then,' she said very quietly.

I didn't know whether I should be hurt by that, but it was more interesting to wonder why she had wanted to go to the temple at all. Because she believed that the long-limbed god, wet with the milk and honey they poured on him, understood and kept track of everything? *Even the fall of a sparrow* – that's what one of the nuns at school had once said, her face shining with adoration.

When I went into Janaki's room one morning she was sitting before the big iron trunk I had seen in the storeroom. The room was, as usual, warmer, darker and more closed than the rest of the house. She must have dragged or carried the trunk in by herself. I had already discovered that she was strong for someone so slight, that her hands were especially large, firm and in control. She was crouching before the trunk and opening it with a key that was not part of a bunch. She flung open the lid and it fell back noiselessly when she looked up and saw me. I wanted to stay and see what was inside, but I knew she would send me downstairs now.

But no: she said, 'Stay if you want to,' and I sat down to watch.

There were three silver vesels inside the trunk – two very small bowls and a spoon. They had been placed over a sari that might have been one of Janaki's wedding saris.

'Are they yours?' I couldn't help asking.

'Yes. There were more, but Sundar decided to sell the others two years ago.'

The sari was a simple red and green. The flecks of gold on it had turned dull.

'We'll cut this up later and make something with it. Maybe a pavadai for you,' she said.

I stared at her.

'Will you wear it?' she asked.

I nodded. Yes, I would wear it.

There were other saris below the silk one. Bulkily

112

folded nine-yard saris with the striped and checked pattern I knew older women wore.

'My mother's,' Janaki said. I looked up at the sadness in her voice. I could barely remember my grandmother. What had *she* felt about everything that had happened to Janaki? Sorry for her and for herself. Ashamed. I still had a vague memory of how Amma had cried when the telegram had come informing us of her mother's death two years ago. She had flung herself on the bed and sobbed and it was the only time I had ever seen my father put his arms around her, lost and inadequate in the face of her grief. Janaki wouldn't have cried aloud like that.

'My mother would often tell me that I was born in the hottest month of the year,' Janaki was saying. 'When the ground is on fire. All three of us were born here – right here in this room. But all she could remember of the third time was not the pain, she would say, only the terrible heat.'

The trunk was empty now, except for a few dog-eared college textbooks with Janaki's name on them. I wondered why she had bothered to preserve these. She opened one and took out a flat brown envelope full of photographs. Three children stood downstairs in the front room. One of the two girls was taller than the other and a little more plump; the other was fair and small with two very long plaits thrown over her shoulders. They held their brother's hands, one hand for each of them. Sundar was tall, and as heavy-browed as he was now. When Janaki looked at the photograph she smiled and I wished that the moment would go on for ever, that a silver-grey cocoon could be woven around the room and that she could lay her

113

head against its softness and be at peace. I sat on the floor, with little waves of unexpected tenderness that I didn't know what to do with sweeping over me.

Janaki was now showing me a photograph of a very fat, very bald child dressed in a man's veshti, leaning on a walking stick.

'Your mother has changed, hasn't she?' she smiled.

But Sundar was already beginning to look like the Sundar I knew in the photograph taken in Srinivas Photo Studio, Thiruninravur, May 23rd 1968. Janaki gave it to me and I looked at N. Sundararajan, tall and slim and very serious. A high-school boy who listened to his teachers – most of the time, I decided – who was certain that he was nearly always right, who was sneaky and nervous about his few wrongdoings. I gave the photograph back to Janaki.

'My ears were pierced when I was very small,' Janaki said. 'But because one of them got infected when I was ten years old, my mother took off the earring and took me to the goldsmith to get it pierced all over again. Sundar came with us. I'd told him how frightened I was, and when the goldsmith bent over me with his needle Sundar leaped up and bit his arm. He had to be dragged off by my mother and the shop assistant.'

It was a long story coming from Janaki, and I wondered why she had needed to tell it. But we both laughed when she finished.

I caught a brief glimpse of the very last picture – the full-length snapshot of a man. Janaki barely glanced at it before putting it back in. I knew that it was her husband, and wanted to look at it more than anything else in the world.

'Who is that man?' I wanted to ask. 'I haven't even

asked to know his name. Please tell me – what do you remember of him? Do you think of him at all?'

But she was beginning to repack the trunk. So I asked her instead: 'Are you ever bored?'

She stared at me without speaking. When she did speak her voice was louder than usual.

'I try hard to make something of all this, of all that has happened. I really want to. But it doesn't seem to work.' I wondered if she was talking to herself, if she had forgotten I was in the room, and I wondered why she had opened the trunk and let me look through its contents with her.

She turned the key and looked at me. 'I'm not bored. I'm tired.' She then said, 'I'm tired of this place, this house and everything in it. I'm even tired of myself.'

I stood up. 'No you're not,' I said stubbornly.

Even I didn't know what I meant, and when she looked up at me in surprise I had nothing else to say.

*　　*　　*

The annual ceremony to remember my grandfather's death happened a few days after that. Sundar went the day before to buy whatever they would need.

'Do you want me to get you the list you made last year?' Janaki asked.

'I'll remember,' he said.

She opened the door for her brother and shut it quietly behind him. She then sat down on the kitchen floor to chop potatoes. Every potato fell into neat halves, every half into four more pieces, with faint plops as they were dropped into the vessel of water at her side. Sudha went about her work noiselessly. Neither of them spoke to the other. When Sudha had

115

to speak to Janaki she sounded nervous. But Janaki was as calm as she always was. Only her face had changed a little in the two months I had been here. It had grown a little more pinched and pale, and the half-moons under her eyes had grown darker. But her hair was still long and splendid and it curved down her back as she sat on the floor, a snake that might open its eyes, slither softly down with a wonderful rippling of black scales and slide silently across the room. She looked up just then and saw me watching her, but she bent down again and continued her work as unselfconsciously as before.

Sudha – she too had changed. She had grown up, was more beautiful than before and seemed suddenly taller. She also walked differently, with a slow movement of her waist and hips.

Sundar came back with the special vegetables they would have to cook for the next day, fresh ghee, jaggery and sugar for the sweets, flowers, a bundle of firewood and a brass urn because the one they had used last year had got lost. For me the evening was filled with happy anticipation, like the night before a wedding.

'Will there be many people here tomorrow?' I asked Sudha.

She looked surprised. 'Oh, no! It's going to be a very small ceremony. Just your uncle and aunt, the priest, three other brahmin men and the two of us.'

'No one else?' I was disappointed.

'No. They don't have too many close relatives living around here, you know. Even your mother has come only once or twice for this, I think.'

'Yes, I know.'

'It's not a big thing, Nithya. It happens every year.'

She turned away, not wanting to talk any more. One of her mysterious quiet moods had come over her, something that happened more and more frequently now.

'Why doesn't my father do anything on *his* father's death anniversary, then?' I asked Janaki that night.

'Because he is not the oldest son. You have to be both the oldest child and a son.'

That meant there would be no one to set my own parents' spirits at ease. Not that it really mattered to me then. My amma and daddy were both going to live for ever.

When I woke up the next morning Janaki, Sundar and Sudha had had their baths long before. Sundar propped his new shaving mirror against the window sill and drew a careful V on his forehead with a little twig he had dipped into a cup of red. Tirumalai Vadiyar, the family priest, was as huge as an old piece of furniture and as much at ease in Sundar's house. He'd brought a young assistant with him.

'Padma's daughter!' he roared when Sundar told him who I was. 'Padma's daughter! I knew your mother when she was even younger than you,' he told me. 'She was a very mischievous child – ask her if she wasn't. I also got your amma and appa married!'

When he laughed his stomach jiggled and so did his chest, as fat and smooth as a woman's breasts.

'I am seventy-five years old,' he said and laughed again. I stared at him stonily. What was so funny?

'You must go and have your bath,' Sudha whispered to me.

The ceremony was long and dull. I even got tired of

watching Sundar cough over the smoke and wipe his watering eyes. The younger priest sat up so straight that there was a little pit between his shoulder blades. His eyes were dark and brooding and he seemed to dislike his older companion, who yawned more and more frequently as the morning crept on.

I went in to see what Janaki and Sudha were cooking. The kitchen was fragrant with the smell of hot rice and tamarind, sugar and ghee. My mouth watered.

'You can't eat yet. Not till the three men have finished,' Janaki told me.

The three brahmin men who had to be invited to the feast were Narayan Mama, Gopal and Vasu. They came in a little after the ceremony began, and Sudha and Janaki served them lunch after it was over. Vasu was as quiet as usual, and though Kamala had probably told him to remember everything he saw, heard and ate, he preferred to look dreamily out the window whenever he thought no one would notice. Even Gopal, who was usually not so quiet, seemed uncomfortable and ploughed through his food listlessly, wanting only to get back home to sleep.

'You are eating very little,' Sundar said.

'Gastric problems,' Gopal muttered.

Only Narayan Mama seemed to be truly enjoying himself. Self-assured as ever, he talked endlessly of his trips to Madras, of his plans for the spiritual welfare and cultural vitality of the street, of all the things he believed in and lived for.

'It is important to keep them in touch with our heritage,' he told the priest, who smiled and nodded, his mouth full of rice.

'Look at our young friend here.' He meant the

priest's assistant, 'Very few young men want to do what he is doing any more. They all want government jobs. And in Madras they all want to become engineers.'

The young man didn't look up. He ate very little and finished before everyone else.

Gopal and Vasu left after lunch. I thought Gopal was really beginning to look rather ill. Vasu didn't want to stay longer but it didn't seem like he wanted to go home, either. He clutched the yellow bag containing the coconut, betel leaves and the forty rupees Sundar had given him and stood outside the door uncertainly before unfurling his umbrella and setting off down the road. Only Narayan Mama wanted to stay on. After washing his hands outside, he lingered in the kitchen, in the front room and then at the gate, talking all the while. I wondered if he talked as much to his own family and if they even bothered to listen. Sundar held the gate open for him, his eyelids so heavy that no one could say whether he was listening or bored.

I was getting very hungry. 'I want to eat,' I said. Sudha served me lunch. She and Janaki would eat later, she said.

'I'll be upstairs. Call me when Tirumalai Vadiyar leaves.' Sundar came in to tell us after he had finally seen his last guest off. Janaki had already gone up.

Tirumalai Vadiyar was asleep in the front room. With one arm tucked below his head, his grey beady eyes opening every now and then to blink, he reminded me – just a little – of a kindly old gorilla I had once seen in a zoo. His panchagacham rode up his calves and thighs, which were covered with wrinkles and warts. The younger man sat in a corner of the room reading the newspaper, waiting for Tirumalai Vadiyar to wake up so they could both be paid and he could get home. It looked like everyone had forgotten he was in the house.

I wandered into the kitchen and picked up a sweet. It was still warm between my fingers, and as hard and round as some strange seed. I couldn't remember Amma making it. I sat down by the large container of raw rice, nearly as tall as I was, and leaned my head against its coolness and bit into the sweet. I'd never liked anything as much. They'd told me it was made only at funerals and death ceremonies.

What if I was as greedy as Kodai, ate too much and was ill that night? Or what would happen if I got a toothache and had to have wads of cotton dipped in clove oil stuffed into my mouth? I didn't think there was a dentist in Thiruninravur.

Whoever was talking outside kept their voices low. They were taking care not to wake up the old man. The voices stopped and Sudha came into the kitchen.

'Who were you talking to?' I asked her.

'That young priest. His name is Venkatesh. Do you know he is only seventeen years old? My brother Ananth is going to look like him in some years.'

'But Ananth is not going to be a priest,' I reminded her.

'No, he's not,' she said. She was very certain about that. 'Venkatesh too went to school till his father died.'

She went into the front room carrying a glass of water for him and I followed her because this young man – who, I had discovered earlier when I had peeked into his bag, carried a pair of trousers to change into once he finished his priestly duties –

might be interesting. Though he seemed suspicious of me, he seemed comfortable with Sudha, who asked him about his family. Did he have any brothers? Was he from Thiruninravur?

'What about you?' he then asked. 'I was told that your appa is also a priest.'

'Yes, he is,' Sudha began. She sounded sad. 'He . . .'

Sundar came in just then. I saw him look at Sudha and then at Venkatesh before he spoke to Tirumalai Vadiyar, who had just woken up.

'Did you sleep well?' Sundar asked him.

'Oh, yes. I have no trouble sleeping. Unlike you modern young men.'

'I have no trouble sleeping either,' Sundar said, smiling.

Sudha and I left the room when they began settling accounts. When I looked out again, Tirumalai Vadiyar was standing outside the door with his bag tucked under his arm, struggling with his umbrella. Venkatesh took it from him and opened it.

'The next time I come here it should be for your wedding,' the old man told Sundar.

'My wedding? So you won't visit us before that?' Sundar smiled.

'But it's time you got married, Sundar,' Tirumalai Vadiyar said seriously. 'Your parents would be very worried if they were alive and saw you unmarried.'

He peered into the house at Janaki, who was standing behind her brother. 'I'm sure your sister would agree with me.'

Sundar came straight into the kitchen after the two priests had left. Sudha had supposed they would stay to drink coffee and had lit the stove.

'Was there any need to talk to that young man, Srinivas?' Sundar asked her.

Sudha's eyes widened. 'Venkatesh,' she said.

'Whatever. It doesn't matter.'

She turned back to the stove.

'I asked you something,' Sundar said.

'What do you want me to tell you?' Sudha asked him defiantly. 'Yes, I spoke to him. So what? He reminded me of . . . of home.'

Sundar didn't say anything. He only looked at her from beneath his long woman's eyelashes.

'And Nithya was with me all the while,' Sudha said.

'Don't drag Nithya into this,' Sundar said. He hadn't realized I had been with them. 'You know that no respectable brahmin girl would go up to a strange man and begin talking to him.'

'I know that.'

'You do? And of course someone like you wouldn't care.' Sundar turned and left the room.

Sudha looked up but I could see that she was trembling – just a little. But she didn't run upstairs as I expected her to, though she turned off the stove. I knew she hadn't added sugar to the coffee. No one wanted to drink it that day and it stood there through the evening, little bits of flaky white floating on its surface.

Janaki came into the room so quietly that neither of us heard her. She had been cleaning the front room.

'You heard what my brother said,' she told Sudha. 'He's right.' She hesitated and then spat, 'Why did you have to come here at all? You are filthy. A whore . . .'

She pronounced the word clumsily, as if she had

never ever said it before. She went out to empty whatever she'd swept off the floor.

*   *   *

The garden was cool and fresh after the closeness and heat inside. I decided I would stay out as long as they allowed me to. The sun set very quickly, it was there one minute and gone the next, leaving the garden a thicket of moving shadows. I hadn't realized how many different kinds of darkness there were: pitch black, the dark grey of the sky as it was now, the pale watery grey between the darker patches and blobs the leaves threw on the ground. And during the day there were different kinds of green – the dark-almost-black green of mango and jackfruit leaves, the dusty grey-green of the guavas, the light-green-mixed-with-white of the scales on the skins of snake gourds.

I looked back at the house. It didn't look like any of the lights were on inside, but I knew they were not asleep. They had only shut themselves in for the evening. Perhaps Sudha and Sundar had made up their quarrel and were together again. I wanted to know, but didn't want to go in right now to check on them.

'Sudha likes him very much,' I thought, because I still found the idea of love embarrassing, slightly ridiculous. 'Though she was angry with him this evening.'

Maybe she liked him because he made her feel pretty and desirable even though she was a servant, the daughter of a poor priest. And because he was handsome and had been to college. And because Sudha liked big things, adventure. Hadn't she been excited, at least initially, on the day we both got lost though she had let herself be upset by the things that happened later? Maybe, I thought, she was really only a stupid little girl who wasn't yet sure of what she was doing. Maybe that's how the high-school girls at St Mary's – the sports captains and house leaders – really were. Beneath their smart jackets and skirts and swinging hair.

And how would I, Nithya, look and think and feel when I was as old as Sudha was now? I decided that I would never, ever be confused, never be frightened of anything. If I remembered to make sure of that, if I remembered to slightly despise everyone and everything in the world, things would be all right. I felt relieved at the thought of how comfortable and wonderful my own life was going to be. It seemed the only possibility as I sat there on the washing stone that evening beginning to feel a little hungry.

I then thought about Sundar. I had never ever got to know him well enough. He and Janaki were very like each other, and unlike Amma they were tight and closed and mysterious. I wasn't sure how he felt about Sudha. Sridhar had wondered if Sundar went to prostitutes. Though, I reminded myself, that was just another of the stupid things Sridhar sometimes let himself think about. But Sundar didn't want to marry. Everyone thought that strange. Maybe it *was* strange. I couldn't think of any man I knew who wasn't married. My father had been married when he was twenty-eight years old and had grown fatter, balder and even a little nicer over the years, Amma had told me once.

Someone opened and then shut the door to Kodai's house. They had probably finished eating their dinner.

I wondered how Janaki could go without food nearly every night.

Earlier that evening, when I had stayed downstairs after everyone else had gone up to their rooms, Janaki had come down again to refill her jug of water from the pot in the kitchen.

'Is Sudha in her room?' I had called out when she was halfway back up the stairs, only because I wanted to hear her talk about Sudha.

'She is,' she had said, and continued on her way up. She had then stopped again as if she had just thought of something else. I had pretended to be reading.

'I don't want you to spend too much time with Sudha,' Janaki had said.

I had turned a page and asked, without looking up, 'Why not?'

Janaki didn't answer for a minute. 'Because your amma wouldn't want you to,' she had said, and had gone on upstairs.

I had waited till she was almost out of sight. 'I will be friends with whoever I want to, whenever I want to,' I had shouted. Her back had gone stiff. 'And neither you or Amma or even Sundar can stop me.'

I had then come out into the garden glowing with a triumph that already seemed so pointless.

Someone opened the back door and called out for me without switching on a light. It was Janaki. She called without any of the irritation or anxiety I used to hear in Amma's voice when she called me in from play.

Chapter Six

It was the end of March and my birthday. My parents sent me a card showing a maroon camel with a toothy smile and bells around its neck standing against a bright blue sky. *'Greetings from the Desert'* was the message inside. 'For a charming eleven-year-old,' my father had added in red felt-tip pen to go with the colour of the camel's coat. It didn't sound like him at all. I couldn't help wondering why he had written that. It worried me. Was he already beginning to forget me or is that what he hoped I would grow up to be – charming, as easily lovable as other girls?

Amma had written me a letter telling me about the new things she was seeing – the buildings, the bright lights, the sand dunes and the music. 'It sometimes feels like Bombay. I wish you were with us.' She also said that she'd got me new clothes, made in America and Hong Kong, and would give them to me as soon as she got back. 'But if you've grown much taller they won't fit you. Have you grown much taller? Write more often. We have received only one letter from you in nearly three months.'

I felt guilty when I read that. She was right – I hadn't bothered to write as often as I should have. My poor Amma, who seemed to love me so much, and my father, who had been going to work day after day after day for as long as I could remember. It was not that I didn't *like* writing to them; it was just that there was so much else happening.

'Dear Amma and Daddy,' I wrote. 'I am fine. I do hope you both are in the best of health. Thank you for the card. I just received it.'

That was how I began every letter I wrote for English Composition class. I chewed at the end of my fountain pen, hoping it would begin to leak and they would have to get me a new one, and tried to think of what else there was to say. How I had seen Sundar slipping into Sudha's room at night? The things Kodai had told me? How Sridhar wanted to see Sudha having her bath, Raghu and his stupid passion for Janaki and how lonely Janaki was and how tired? What would my parents do if they read that? Come straight back home on the next flight, not even caring to make sure the company paid for their tickets, and take me back to Bangalore, home and St Mary's.

'Don't worry too much about me,' I continued, 'though I am really very bored a lot of the time, because as you told me very little happens here. But I have my books to keep me occupied.' ('How well you write!' Amma would exclaim in her next letter. 'You are beginning to sound so grown up . . .')

I went to look for Janaki. 'I got a letter from my mother. She asked after you.'

Janaki seemed to have decided not to let our exchange over my being friends with Sudha bother her, though I knew she couldn't have forgotten it. I had been waiting for her to bring up the matter once more, perhaps one night when we were alone together, but she never did. Her manner with Sudha hadn't changed after that evening, either. She continued giving her instructions in her usual calm, steady voice and worked silently alongside her in the kitchen and around the house. I sometimes wondered if that afternoon had really happened, if Sundar and Janaki had really said all those things.

But I found that my decision to defy Janaki and continue spending time with Sudha was really pointless, because Sudha herself seemed to have decided to keep her distance. She grew completely withdrawn, even from me. She began to wake up long before everyone else, so that when the rest of us came down she'd already done most of the work and gone back up. I never found out if Sundar still continued visiting her at night, though I couldn't think of any reason for him to stop. Because I was nearly always around when the two of them were together, though they didn't always know it, I also knew that Janaki hadn't said anything more to Sudha. But Sudha had changed.

I went up to her room one afternoon. She had shut the door, something she had hardly ever done before. She wanted us to know that she did not want to be disturbed. So I went back downstairs and switched on the radio. Only Sundar listened to the radio, and then never very loudly, but now there was nothing to listen to – news on one station and film music on another. I pushed the glowing orange line up and down and the radio murmured, hissed and crackled. I switched it off, went back up the stairs and knocked at Sudha's door. Sudha must have heard me, because when I placed my ear against the door I heard her moving inside. But she didn't reply, and when I listened again the sounds had stopped. She was pretending to be asleep, hoping that whoever was outside would go away. I knocked again, louder this time.

'Who's there?' she asked.

'It's me,' I said.

'What do you want?'

That was a game I had played with my friends many years ago.

Knock knock.

Who's there?

It's me.

What do you want?

And then there would be a monster, a misshapen goblin, a wild-haired witch standing outside waiting to be let in.

'What do you want?' Sudha asked again. Her voice sounded strange and I wondered if she had been crying.

'Open the door for me.'

She came out and stood at the entrance. She was barring the way and I wondered why she bothered to do that. I'd been inside her room just a few days ago, when she was away, and it had looked as it always did – the mirror with three of the maroon felt bindis I had given her stuck on it, the mattress, the tin trunk locked and placed against the wall. I had stood right in the middle of the room and sniffed for new smells I hadn't detected before. But there was only the crisp scent of half-dry leaves from outside. Sudha always left her windows open.

'Let's go downstairs,' I said.

'Why?' she asked suspiciously.

'Why? So that we can do something together.' I tried to sound hurt.

She looked doubtful.

'Why don't you want to talk to me all of a sudden?' I asked. 'Do you know how boring it is for me out here? I wish they had taken me with them to Kuwait, I wish I was back home, I wish . . .' I was surprised at the intensity of my sudden rage and resentment. Why was I saying all this?

Sudha laid her hand on my shoulder. Her face was pale and dry, the smooth skin stretched tight across it like a sheet. Only her eyes were large, dark and soft. She took her hand off and looked down at me as if she didn't know what to say.

'Why don't you want to talk to me?' I asked again sullenly. I was determined that she answer.

'It's better that you don't talk to me,' she said.

Before I could say anything she went on: 'Better for you, I mean. Your Janaki Chitti is right – you shouldn't spend too much time with me.'

'Is she saying that because she thinks of you as a servant?' Just for a minute I was shocked at how deceitful I could be – I sounded like Kodai talking to her parents in her high baby-girl voice.

Sudha hadn't expected me to say that. She looked at me carefully.

'Maybe that's why,' she said at last.

'Only because of that?' I wanted to ask. 'Are Janaki and Sundar worried that you will corrupt me? Like our great-grandparents were afraid of being defiled by bodies that might bump against their own, and even by passing shadows?'

But I didn't say anything. I stood at her door and looked up at her.

'Come downstairs,' I begged at last. And I really wanted her to come and chatter the afternoon away as I leafed languidly through the pages of my books, or to take a bus with me and get lost in an adventure she would truly enjoy this time. But she shook her head. 'You are still a child. It's better for you this way. You don't understand.' That was all she would say.

But I knew that she stood at her door and watched me as I turned away and went through the storeroom and down the stairs. As if she were seeing me off on a journey she couldn't take herself.

So, except for one more afternoon, I spent very little time with Sudha after that. She had withdrawn to a place where I couldn't reach her, where the cleverest of my questions couldn't probe. I spent many hours wondering what she was thinking and feeling. I resented the fact that I couldn't fully understand what was happening around me. For the first time ever, I was aware that I was so much younger than everyone else around me and that I knew less about certain things than even Kodai.

*   *   *

There was suddenly very little to do. The days were long and unbearably still. I didn't want to go over to the neighbours' house and see Kodai. She would ask me questions I didn't want to answer or didn't know the answers to.

'It's so dull here . . . it's so *dull* . . .' I whined to myself again and again, wishing that Amma was around to hear me and to feel guilty about having left me behind. I was sometimes seized by the need to run upstairs and bang furiously at Sudha's door. It would make all three of them come out of their rooms and I imagined them standing around, looking at me in bewilderment. But I didn't do it. I only sat in the front room for hours, waiting for either Janaki or Sudha to come down or for Sundar to return or for the sound of voices upstairs.

I had seen Janaki cutting up the material for the skirt she had promised to make me out of her sari, but I hadn't seen her working at the sewing machine. I decided to ask her about it even though I didn't particularly like wearing pavadais. I wore them only when Amma insisted, to weddings and sometimes to the temple.

'Where is that pavadai you started on?' I asked Janaki just before we went to bed one night.

She frowned. So she had forgotten all about it. 'Which one?'

'The one you said you'd make for me out of that sari.'

'Oh, that one,' Janaki said, 'I decided not to make it. The silk is old and hasn't been looked after. It tears easily.'

I didn't really care, but I persisted. 'I thought I saw you cutting it up.'

'Yes, but I threw it away after that. It might be wrong to give you a skirt made with that sari – I don't know if your amma and appa would want you to wear it. It might bring bad luck and you know I wouldn't want to pass any of that on to you.'

132

I believe Janaki actually started to be quite fond of me at around that time.

* * *

April 14th, New Year's Day, fell on a Friday. Sundar left for Madurai on Thursday evening. No one knew that he even meant to go till he came down dressed for the office on Thursday morning, carrying a suitcase with him. Janaki must have been surprised and I waited for her to ask Sundar if he was going somewhere straight from work, but she did not.

It was only when he was wheeling his scooter out the door that he told us, 'I'm going out of town this evening – to Madurai.'

Sudha came out of the kitchen wiping her hands on her sari. I looked at her carefully to see if her face fell or if she was even the least bit disappointed. Though she seemed unmoved, I could see that she was waiting for Sundar to say something more, her straight black brows gathered together in a very slight frown.

'I am going with my colleagues Ravi and Srikanth. We are visiting the Meenakshi temple,' Sundar added when he came back in for his suitcase. Janaki nodded, and I wondered if she was upset that he hadn't told her about this trip earlier. Sundar looked swiftly around the room to see if he had left anything behind.

'All right, then.' He nodded to us and turned to go.

Sudha stepped towards him. I was startled. What's going to happen now? I thought. Is she going to stop him? Or insist that he take her along?

But she only asked, 'When are you coming back?'

Janaki stared at her, and Sundar too seemed surprised. I knew that it was not just the unexpectedness of Sudha going up to Sundar and addressing him in Janaki's and my presence – it was the sudden despair in Sudha's eyes. It shocked even me.

'On Sunday,' was all Sundar said before he left.

Janaki and I watched him riding away, the suitcase placed securely between his legs. He would probably leave the scooter at one of his friends' houses for the weekend. It hadn't ever been important for him to tell his sister or perhaps even Sudha about his plans. None of us knew anything about his days at the office or his frequent trips to his land at the village, and we had no idea if he went anywhere else or did other things. His life seemed big and grand to me, especially when compared to the littleness of Janaki's and Sudha's.

I followed Janaki back into the house.

'Remember to add more salt to the sambhar before Nithya has her lunch,' Janaki told Sudha. She looked at her very carefully, as if there were things she too needed to know.

That evening she asked me if I would like anything special cooked for the New Year – vadai and payasam, maybe.

'No,' I said firmly. 'I hate them.' Vadais that dripped oil into my mouth when I bit into them had always disgusted me, and I especially couldn't bear the thought of eating them when it was so hot outside.

'Then tell Sudha not to get anything ready for tomorrow.'

'What if Sudha wants something nice to eat, something special?' I asked.

'I don't think she'll want anything,' Janaki replied. I decided not to argue. But after I had passed on

Janaki's message to Sudha, I asked her if she wanted anything special for the New Year lunch.

'No,' she said without looking up from whatever she was doing.

The holiday was being celebrated more conspicuously at Kodai's house. When I went out after lunch, I saw guests coming out into the backyard to wash their hands after what must have been one of Kamala's big lunches. Even after they went in and shut the door I could hear the sounds of talking and laughter. Till some time ago, Sudha would have come to sit with me on the washing stone to watch and wonder how many guests had been invited and what Kamala had cooked for them. I would have made mean comments about how much Kodai had probably eaten and Sudha would have laughed. I had always been able to make Sudha laugh.

That morning the three of us, Janaki, Sudha and me, had clustered before the gods on the kitchen shelf, and Sudha had lit the lamp and a disc of camphor to mark the beginning of the new year. Janaki had dipped her head for just a minute before going upstairs. But Sudha had kept her eyes shut tight for a long while, her lips moving in a prayer I couldn't hear. Two little spots of lamplight fell on her face and I thought how beautiful she still was in spite of everything, with her perfect nose with its speck of gold, her large eyes and her full, half-child's-half-woman's mouth. She prayed for a long time. After she died, and now much later still, that is one of the things that I remember most vividly about her: her face shining, praying that somehow things would be altered and that as she stumbled on helplessly someone would

135

break her fall. Someone very powerful, very forgiving and very good.

I sat in the garden that afternoon for quite a while. Kodai came out into her backyard followed by two smaller girls dressed in what looked like new clothes. Each wore two plaits folded up and tied with ribbons. I thought they both looked a little frightened of Kodai, but they trotted after her obediently as she walked heavily through the trees. She turned around every now and then to give them instructions I couldn't hear.

'They're playing some stupid little game,' I thought. But I caught myself feeling almost envious.

I remembered the first conversation I had ever had with Kodai, right here in Sundar's backyard, and wondered if she was telling the two little girls the things she had told me then. I tried to imagine what *they* would do. They looked like timid little things; they would probably run up to their mother and blurt everything out.

'And wouldn't it serve Kodai right!' I exulted.

Someone had got into our own garden – I could hear the leaves crackle somewhere behind me.

It must be Raghu again, I thought. Though I was beginning to think he was really quite nice, after the day he'd helped Sudha and me get home, I wished he wouldn't come here. But I also suspected that it wasn't like him to enter the garden. He might hover around the bushes once in a while but he wouldn't come in without permission.

I'd better go and check who it is, I thought. What if it's a thief, or someone who has found out that Sundar is away for the weekend?

Two boys crawled through the undergrowth. They

were both a little older than I was, but it wasn't hard to see that they didn't belong to this neighbourhood. They were wearing loincloths, and their legs were so stringy that I couldn't believe they could actually support the weight of their bodies. Their skin was reddish-brown, and when I got closer I saw the grey-green patterns of the tattoos on their arms. They both carried catapults made of clumsily cut wood and strips of rubber. I knew that I had only to step out and show myself to them and they would turn and run in a flash. But I decided to go in and fetch Sudha.

I pushed her door open, since it wasn't latched from the inside this time. I paused to take note of what she was doing. She was doing nothing, just sitting crouched on her bed, her head bent low. She started when she saw me.

'Come quickly. There are two people – I don't know who they are – in the garden,' I said. But when we reached the trees they had disappeared. Maybe they had seen me going in and decided it was safer to leave. But Sudha was quicker than I was.

'There they are!' She ran forward so fast that I had trouble keeping up with her. The boys had raised their catapult and were aiming at something I couldn't see, something above us on the gooseberry tree.

'What do you want here?' Sudha shouted. They ran between the trees with her following, then swiftly vaulted over some bushes and disappeared.

'They've gone!' She came back to where I stood, panting. It had been a long time since I'd seen such excitement on her face.

But they had hit whatever they had shot at. We heard a low squeak behind us.

'It's a bird,' I said, and we scrambled in the grass looking for it. It was a very young squirrel, grey with the three white lines Sri Rama had stroked down its back with the tips of his fingers. A little blood trickled down its side and at first we thought it was dead, but when Sudha bent over and touched it gently with the back of her hand, it struggled to run in a flurry of panic. It couldn't move more than a few inches, and when it got to my feet it rolled over on its side and went still. I looked at, bewildered. How suddenly it had died! When I crouched down on the ground I could see that the beady eyes were not quite shut, and when I peered into the open mouth I could see a grey-pink tongue and tiny sharp teeth. The patch of spiky fur above one of the legs was covered with brownish blood that was already beginning to dry. Sudha was stroking it softly.

'Poor thing,' she said, and she hunched her shoulders together and shivered as if she were cold.

'Are we going to leave it here?' I asked.

'No, we'll bury it.'

We dug a grave for it beneath a bush.

'It has to be a little deep. The cats shouldn't be able to get at it,' Sudha said. We lined the grave with leaves and just when we were about to put the squirrel in, I was seized by panic. What if it wasn't *really* dead, what if it was only unconscious or something and would wake up suddenly and find itself buried? I imagined it opening its eyes, gasping for breath and frantically trying to dig its way out but not even being able to move in the narrow bed of leaves we had made for it.

'Are you sure it's *completely* dead?' I asked Sudha.

'Of course it is.' She was certain.

'Have you seen a dead animal before?'

'No. But I know this one is dead.' And she pushed the mud over it and flattened the earth with the flat of her hand.

'Poor thing,' she said again. 'Why did they have to get at this one of all the other things out here?

I had hoped she would stay out a little longer but she didn't, stopping only at the pump to wash her hands and muddy feet.

*   *   *

I waited to see if Sundar's return from Madurai would make a difference to Sudha. I too was beginning to think of his return as something big, an event that would mark the start of something important. Besides, any kind of change, however trivial, was welcome to me over that long weekend, with Janaki as silent as ever and Sudha continuing to keep to herself after the episode with the squirrel.

On Friday night I took out the pocket calendar I'd got with a pack of toothpaste and marked out the days since I had come to Thiruninravur with blue crosses. January 20th to April 14th – that was nearly three months. The uncrossed dates stared back at me – three more months to go. They were long and hot and stretched on for ever. I threw myself on my bed and burst into tears. I couldn't stay here much longer, I thought, I would die if I stayed here much longer. I needed to get out of this house, jump over the bushes like those two boys had done and run swiftly down the back road. I heard my feet thump on the ground and felt the breeze on the back of my neck and in my ears.

I got up to push Janaki's curtains aside, because that was all I could do. But then I heard her coming up the stairs, ducked back into bed and pulled the sheet over my head. My eyes were probably swollen with crying and I didn't want her to ask me any questions. Though, I reminded myself, she was not likely to. Only Amma would panic if she happened to come into my room and catch me in tears.

I tried to remember the reasons I had had for crying back home and couldn't. I didn't quite know why I had cried just now either. Was it simply because there was nothing to do? I only knew that I hadn't cried so much for a very long time. When I laid my cheek on my pillow again it was wet.

The next morning, when I came down for coffee, I found Janaki talking to Sudha. 'You could have gone home to see your mother for the New Year,' she was saying. 'You can still go if you want to, and return later in the week.'

I waited for Sudha to answer and knew that Janaki was waiting too. That was why she had made the offer to begin with, to see what Sudha would say. When Sudha didn't reply, Janaki added, 'I'll give you the money for the bus fare if you need it.'

'No, I don't want to go home.'

And because I was standing by her side pouring out coffee I heard Sudha's voice shake. I also saw something as soft as a shadow flit softly across Janaki's face – anger or disapointment or something else.

When I opened the front door that afternoon I saw a letter that the postman had thrust between the gate and the wall. This one was a postcard, written in Tamil and postmarked Thirukullam – Sudha's village.

I peered closely at the writing but couldn't yet make anything of it. I went up to Sudha's room to give it to her. She wasn't there, though she hadn't been down in the kitchen either. I found her sitting under the spreading shade of the tamarind. Just like the other day when I had opened her door, she was doing nothing – just sitting. I was surprised at how heavy and dull she looked.

'It's a letter for you. I think it's from your father.'

She jumped up and turned away. She seemed frightened and I thought she would refuse to take it from me. But she stretched out her hand and quickly ran her eyes over the small, neat, blue-inked words. She then brushed past me and ran inside and up to her room. I followed but she banged the door shut behind her.

Janaki came out of her room. She had heard the thud of our footsteps as we ran up.

'Has something happened?' she asked.

I wondered if she was surprised to see me standing, panting and slightly sweat-streaked, outside Sudha's closed door.

'Nothing,' I said. I went back downstairs.

I managed to get hold of that postcard after Sudha died. Many years after that, when I had really learnt to read Tamil, I worked my way through it and understood why it had upset Sudha. When was she coming home next? her father wanted to know. Ananth was doing well at school and they thought they'd nearly found a groom for Kausalya but his family had wanted more money and a bigger wedding than they could afford. Sudha's amma was always, always thinking of her, the letter ended – just last night she had been telling Sudha's father that she was the cleverest of the three girls. They would never forget how much she was helping them out by working for Sundar and Janaki.

* * *

Late that evening, only because there was nothing else to do, I wandered out to look at Lakshmi. She was standing in her shed, placidly twitching her tail at the fat black flies that darted and lunged around her. Sudha had finished milking her. I had seen the foaming vessels in the kitchen. I clicked my tongue at Lakshmi, as I had seen Sudha do. But she looked at me indifferently and settled down for the night with a great clatter of hoofs on the stone ground. There was nothing for me to do here, either.

I thought I would go in and look for something to eat, but I had to clean my feet first because something was sticking to my soles – mud or a bit of dried dung. There were some vessels around the pump waiting to be washed, so I would have to go over to the bathroom instead.

I pushed open the door and didn't realize immediately that Sudha was in there. She had put her lamp in a corner, and the flame hissed and spluttered when drops of water fell on it. In the dim light I saw that she had taken off her sari but still had on her blouse and underskirt, and she was pouring water over her head as though she were having a bath. Her loosened hair had fallen over her face and stuck to it in straight, wet black strands through which I could see her eyes. I felt a thrill of fear. It was as if she was mad.

She almost seemed naked because the water made

142

her skirt stick to her long legs and outlined the curved bones of her hips, her flat stomach and her rounded breasts under the cheap cotton of her blouse and underclothes. I wanted to reach out and touch her. I knew that this was what Sundar and the men on the street who looked at her saw, even when she had a sari on. She pushed her hair back and saw me standing at the door, but she didn't seem embarrassed or even surprised. She just stood there looking at something behind my shoulder with dull, quiet eyes. I turned and fled.

I lay in bed that night and tried to imagine how *I* would look when I was twenty years old. I dreamt that I had become Sudha or Janaki or both of them at once. I dismantled myself as if I were a jigsaw puzzle, threw out some pieces and put in new ones. A bunch of people were watching me because it was important to wait and see what new pattern would emerge at the end. And then I was standing thigh-deep in a large, flat field of water. Someone I didn't know called out for me, and when I waded towards them I was dismayed to see blood trickle down my legs and spread around in gently widening circles, turning the water red.

I woke up with a start. Amma had been vaguely anxious about just this before she left. I slipped out of the room and ran downstairs to the kitchen and switched on the light to check. But when I pulled out my underpants they were as clean and unspotted as ever. I went back to sleep feeling tremendously relieved. When I woke up the next morning I couldn't remember if I had had more dreams or even finished that one.

Sunday seemed less long and tortuous. The sun was

out and the sky was cloudless and blinding blue, but it wasn't as hot as it had been over the week and would be again after that. I decided to drop my vigil temporarily and stop thinking about everything.

But when I heard Sundar come in the next morning, I ran downstairs. He must have got back by the early-morning train – I had already looked it up in the railway timetable I had found downstairs. He had picked up his scooter from his friend's house and come home for a bath and food before going to work. He didn't say anything about his trip, and neither Sudha nor Janaki asked him. I hung around in the kitchen waiting impatiently for my turn to eat. Just once I caught Sundar looking at Sudha carefully. Surely he couldn't not notice how different she looked – the dullness in her eyes and face – or miss the lifelessness with which she moved. But I couldn't guess at what he felt. Surprise? Concern? Or nothing at all? He got up, washed his hands and left the house, shutting the door heavily behind him.

Sudha was restless and on edge that day, as though she were waiting for something. She didn't go upstairs after she had finished her work; instead she swept and watered the area in front of the house for the second time that day and cleaned the front room and the kitchen, scraping at the thin layer of grease on the stove and wiping with soap and water the circles of oil left by vessels and bottles. She even took down the aluminium and steel containers of lentils, powders and spices and dusted the shelves. This is why, when people came into the house the day she died and the day after, they marvelled at its tidiness.

I didn't try to get her to talk. In spite of her sudden

rush of energy, I began to wonder if she was going to fall ill. Her eyes burnt feverishly and she licked her lips every now and then with a quick, nervous movement, as if their dryness bothered her. But in the evening, when it was time for Sundar to return from work, she had another bath, and when she came down again to cook the rice I saw that she had washed her face for the evening, something she hadn't bothered to do for days.

*　　*　　*

That night, after Janaki came up, I went downstairs for a pen to finish a letter to my parents. The kitchen light was on and I saw Sundar standing at the door, his back towards me.

'What's the matter now?' I heard him ask. As he moved into the kitchen and shut the door, I caught a glimpse of Sudha inside. I went farther up the front room and stood in the shadows.

'What's the matter?' Sundar repeated. It wasn't too hard to hear him.

Sudha didn't answer him at once. I waited impatiently. *Maybe she's crying*, I thought, and I crept up to the door – Sundar hadn't shut it fully. She wasn't crying. She was standing in the middle of the kitchen and looking at him when he lost his temper, strode up to her and shook her. I had never seen Sundar this way before.

'Why don't you say something?' he asked roughly. 'Have you swallowed your tongue or what?'

Later I would try very often to remember every detail of this conversation. People asked me so many questions about so many different things that whatever I

145

heard that night began to dance around my head in twisted little circles. But sometimes when I was alone, I remembered nearly everything each of them had said – very distinctly.

When she told Sundar that she knew something was wrong, that she might be going to have a child, I wondered if I had heard right.

'What do you mean?' Sundar asked. And though I couldn't see his face I could imagine his jaw slackening like that of a figure in a cartoon strip, his eyes big and suddenly very stupid.

'He is frightened,' I thought.

Sudha looked up at him steadily, and when she spoke again she seemed to be in control of herself. 'What do you think we can do about it?' she asked.

'I don't know.'

'You realize that something has to be done about it?'

My legs were cramped from crouching outside the door, and I wasn't even allowing myself to breathe loudly. I knew that when I got up I would sneeze or my legs would be heavy with pins and needles, making it impossible for me to get upstairs fast enough. I desperately wanted them to settle things as quickly as possible. It couldn't be as complicated as all that.

'Nothing can be done about it,' Sundar said firmly. He didn't sound afraid any longer – he had simply made up his mind. Sudha seemed to understand that and it seemed to frighten her. Her eyes widened as if she had seen something dreadful pushing its way out of a nightmare.

'I can get rid of the child, can't I?'

'No, you can't. Not here, anyway.'

'Why not?'

He looked at her as if she had gone mad. 'Of course you can't do it here. Everyone knows me – there would be a terrible scandal.'

'Is that all you can think about?' she asked.

'I also have my widowed sister's reputation to think of,' he said stiffly, 'and Padma's daughter is under my care now. And what about you? Aren't you worried about people talking about you? Or doesn't that matter to you any more?' He spoke deliberately, as if he were willing himself to be cruel. So that he could stop seeing Sudha as a real person, so that his own world would be less complicated.

They talked for what seemed a very long while. I wanted it all to end and for all of us to be able to go back to sleep. Sundar spoke calmly and very softly, Sudha fought like a small wounded animal making its bid for life. She asked him for money; she would make the arrangements herself. But hadn't he already told her the abortion wasn't a good idea? She would go somewhere else – to Madras. And what would she do in a big city – a village girl like her?

'You can come with me.'

'I will not.'

'Why can't you? You've been to these places before, haven't you? I thought you were a big man, a man of the world,' she spat. 'Why can't you come?'

He seemed puzzled, as if even he didn't know why. But when he spoke again it was with an air of finality: 'I will not.'

She sat down on the floor, as though she were tired. Sundar crouched by her side. 'You should go home,' he said, more gently this time.

She looked up at him incredulously.

'You can go home – your parents will take care of you – and you know they won't talk about this to anyone else.'

'You know I can't go home!' She sprang up, trembling all over. 'I'll die before I go home.'

'Be sensible and listen to me. Go home.' Sundar stood up and turned around. I could see his face now.

She came close to where he stood and looked at him with such hatred in her eyes that even he seemed shaken. 'I was a fool,' she snarled. 'And you are a coward. You will never know just how much I – *despise* you.'

Sundar shrugged. 'I'll draw some money from my bank tomorrow. You can leave by the end of this week,' was all he said, and he came towards the door.

I stepped back quickly and stood close against the wall so he didn't see me when he came out and went up the stairs. I hadn't looked up to see if anyone else had been listening, but because the night was so still, anyone standing at the bottom of the stairs could have heard them and also seen me.

I didn't go in to Sudha. After waiting for a few mintues to make sure Sundar was safely back in his room, I too went to bed.

Chapter Seven

After Sudha died it became important for the neighbours to remember the last time they had seen or spoken to her. Kamala told many people, many times over, how she had had a long chat with Sudha just a day before she died.

'Just think of that!' she would say. 'She'd probably made up her mind already when she spoke to me – *if* she really killed herself, that is.' That last bit was usually added in a cautious whisper.

Kamala also liked to say that she had sensed something was terribly wrong. 'I sensed something was terribly wrong. The girl was frightened, in fact she came close to *telling* me she was frightened! It was just that I felt it wasn't right to ask too many questions about whatever was happening at the neighbours' house.' And whoever she happened to be talking to would nod with understanding and sympathy, wishing that they had been there too.

But very little of what Kamala said was true. I had been with Sudha when Kamala spoke to her. I was looking out of an upstairs window when I saw Sudha go out into the garden, and I slipped out to join her. I had been thinking about whether to tell her that I had overheard her conversation with Sundar the night before, but decided not to because she seemed quite calm now. She was neither heavy, dull nor hysterically excited as she had alternately been over the last few weeks. She came purposefully out of Lakshmi's shed carrying a broom and a basket of damp, dung-splattered straw.

'Why have you finished so early?' I asked.

'Because I'm going out later this afternoon,' she said, and she went to empty the basket in the big cement bin in a corner of the compound.

The dark swirls under her eyes were the only signs that something was bothering her. They also made her look like Janaki. Her shoulders suddenly seemed very narrow, the bones more prominent than before – Sudha had become thinner without any of us really noticing. I glanced at her stomach furtively. It was flat, in spite of the bunched-up folds of the sari, and I remembered how smooth and wet it had been that night in the bathroom beneath the fine cloth of her skirt. I had seen pregnant women before – they all had had swollen faces and fat, rounded stomachs that looked like they had been precariously attached to their bodies as a mean afterthought.

'She has made a mistake,' I thought. 'She's not going to have a child after all.' I didn't know what made women believe they were pregnant to begin with. That was one more thing I had to look up somewhere.

Sudha came back to wash her feet.

'Where are you going?' I asked her. 'I can come with you.'

'No, I want to go by myself,' she said quickly, but she turned and smiled. She wanted to let me know that she didn't mean to hurt me.

It was then that Kamala loomed into view on the side of the bushes. 'Is that you, Janaki?' she called cheerfully.

I saw Sudha stand quite still. I thought she was going to pretend not to have heard Kamala and go straight into the house, but Kamala didn't give her a chance.

'Oh, it's you!' she said, and she squeezed herself clumsily through the largest gap between bushes.

'Let her get stuck there,' I prayed, 'or at least let her tear her stupid sari.'

But Kamala emerged unscathed and came up to where we stood. 'I haven't seen you for a long time. Is everything all right?'

Sudha nodded. Kamala looked curiously at the house, with its small, quiet windows and tightly shut kitchen door.

'I heard that Sundar went to Madurai last week. Is that true?'

'Yes, he went there for three days.'

'We have relatives in Madurai – my husband's cousins – but we have never visited them. They don't invite us, he says, but the truth is that he hates to travel,' she sighed. 'And anyway, train fares are so expensive nowadays.'

Kodai must have heard our voices, as she soon came out to join us. She lurked behind her mother's large backside and nodded and winked at me.

What does she want with me *now*? I thought in disgust.

'And how is poor Janaki?' That was always how Kamala, bursting with good food and contentment, insisted on referring to Janaki.

'She's fine,' Sudha said.

'Amma, Amma! Where have you disappeared to?' Sridhar too had come out into the backyard.

'I'm here – at Sundar's house,' Kamala called to him.

'You haven't ironed my shirt. I thought I told you last night that—' He stopped short when he saw Sudha.

'I'll come and do it for you right away.' Kamala smiled at the two of us and followed her son.

Kodai stayed behind. 'Want to come to my house?' she whispered to me, looking to see if Sudha was listening.

'For what?' I thought I might go if there was nothing else to do.

'To play, of course. We'll find something nice to do,' she said with a meaningful smile.

'I can't come. I'm going out with Sudha,' I said, and I walked away. Sudha had already gone in.

That's all that happened when Kamala spoke to Sudha the day before she died.

* * *

I still can't forget how hot it was those few days. I have not had to live through such a summer since. Everyone was talking about the heat, not only because there was nothing else to discuss but because it was impossible not to talk about this monster with searing eyes and burning tail, against which our two-decade-old fans and glasses of buttermilk were so completely ineffectual. Those who could not or would not wear sandals and went out into the main road had melting tar stick to the soles of their feet and spent the rest of the day tenderly touching their ugly little blisters. And there were other things to worry about, I learnt – wells were beginning to dry, and those who still owned fields were growing anxious. Power cuts were more and more frequent, leaving us sweaty, angry and blind every evening. I kept close track of the district's temperature with horrified fascination: it crept relentlessly upwards from 34 to 36 to 40 degrees.

'How much longer will this go on? How much longer?' I asked myself every day, since there was no one else to talk to any more.

*   *   *

I began to feel drowsy at around one o'clock the afternoon after Kamala's visit. The thought of spreading myself out on the floor and looking at the deliciously vague, floaty pictures behind my closed eyelids was tempting. The house suddenly seemed peaceful and kind.

'Maybe everything will be all right after all,' I thought.

But I had to stay up to see in which direction Sudha went, and whether she took anything with her. So I picked up the book of puzzles I'd got just before I left home and began half-heartedly working on the first one. I soon heard Sudha's door open and heard her moving about, but when she didn't come downstairs even after five minutes, I thought I should go up and look.

Her room was empty. I went over to Sundar's room, making sure I walked as quietly as I could. His door was shut, as it always was when he was out, but when I placed my ear against it I could hear someone moving. I decided to risk nudging the door open to see what Sudha – it had to be Sudha – was doing. It opened with the slightest of creaks, which only I could have heard. Sudha had the chest of drawers open and was looking through Sundar's papers. She was in a hurry but didn't seem nervous about someone coming in and catching her. A scooter horn blared outside and she went to the window and looked out. When she came back she crouched on the floor and pulled out a file. I knew there was no point in her doing that. There were only bills and certificates in there, and most of them were in English. I watched her bend over the sheets of papers, frowning.

'There is nothing in there!' I wanted to whisper across the room. 'Don't waste your time – there is nothing in there that can tell you anything worth knowing.'

She rearranged things and put the file back in its place before she pulled open the topmost drawer and took out a roll of currency notes. There didn't seem to be much money in there that day. She hesitated, then took the entire lot, rolled it up, tucked it into her waist and shut the drawer. She tried the bottom drawer but it didn't open. It hadn't opened for me, either. She would come out now. I ran downstairs and waited for her.

But she didn't come down for a while. When she did, I saw that she had put on a fresh sari – one of the two that she liked to wear when she went out. She carried a basket in her hand as if she were going to the vegetable market.

'So you're going out?' I asked her.

'Yes.'

'It's very hot outside – you should take an umbrella. Shall I get you one from upstairs?'

'It doesn't matter.'

'Does Janaki know that you're not going to be at home?'

'She's asleep now. But I told her this morning that I'd be going out for a while.'

I couldn't think of anything else to say and went back to my crossword reluctantly. I didn't see why Sudha couldn't take me wherever she was going. Now I would have nothing to do for the rest of the day but wait for her to return. She unlatched the door and turned around to look at me. Her face was pale.

'If I ask you to come with me, will you tell anyone where we went?' she said.

My heart leaped up. 'No I won't,' I promised hurriedly.

'Not even your mama and chitti?'

I shook my head.

'And later – when you get back home – your mother?'

'I *told* you I wouldn't tell anyone.' I was getting impatient. I raced out to wash my face and then went upstairs. I didn't want to go into Janaki's room so I scribbled a note and slipped it below her door: '*I have gone out with Sudha. Will be back before*' – I hesitated – '*sunset.*' I put my name below the message – '*Nithya.*' At least they couldn't complain that I'd gone without letting them know.

The street was empty. No one lounged outside their gates or at their front doors. No one wanted to be out on an afternoon like this. I was exhilarated – in spite of the heat, it felt wonderful to be out of the house with Sudha. I felt sorry for Janaki, who had to stay in the sweltering semi-darkness of her curtained room.

We didn't have to wait too long for a bus that day, and when we boarded, it was less crowded than last time. For a very long time I remembered exactly who the people who saw us getting into the bus were, simply because, for weeks afterwards, they made sure no one else forgot that they had seen Sudha and me. Bhagya, Gopal's wife, was there with her brother, who everyone knew was trying to get Gopal to return the two thousand rupees he had lent him nearly three years before. Bhagya smiled at us. I knew that she expected us to come and sit near her, but though Sudha smiled back, she slipped into a seat up front. I sat next to her and heard Bhagya tell her brother who Sudha and I were.

'I wondered where they were both going,' Bhagya would later say again and again, when everyone else was also wondering and asking me about that day. The fact that she was one of the last people to see Sudha alive gave Bhagya an importance that outglittered even her neighbour Sulochana's diamonds for a while. And though her brother did not recover his loan, he took back a good story to tell his family.

'Do you know where you want to go?' I whispered to Sudha.

She nodded, but kept her eyes fixed on the dusty houses and shops we bumped and rattled past.

'Why did she have to take me with her if she doesn't

156

want to talk, or even let me know where we're going?'
I thought angrily. But the feeling lasted only for a
minute. Sudha's arm was hot against my own, and I
could almost feel the warm blood throbbing under the
smooth brown skin and see something twitch and
jump on the side of her throat just below her ear. I felt
sorry for her.

Because things were not all right after all, I realized.
If I had not been me, if I had been a different kind of
person, I would have reached out and taken her hands
as they lay on her lap and said something, I couldn't
imagine what, but something that might have helped
her, made her feel better. I sometimes feel a pang of
guilt when I think of that last bus ride together and
wonder if I could have made a difference somehow, if I
could have averted what happened the next day.

'Probably not,' I told myself again and again, and
liked to think that I wasn't entirely wrong.

We got off the bus and into an auto-rickshaw. The
streets looked vaguely familiar – we were on the way
to the temple. But we went straight ahead past it, past
the long-distance bus stand where Sudha caught the
bus to her village. The lanes behind the bus stand were
narrow and lined with small shops and houses. I was
beginning to discover that that's how much of the
town outside GC Street seemed to look. Sudha stopped
the rickshaw at the end of one lane, and I watched her
pay the driver with notes from the bundle she'd taken
from Sundar's room, all tens and fives. I knew that she
had very little money of her own. Sundar sent her
wages home to her father after he had given her thirty
rupees for herself.

The lanes were as empty as our own street had been

when we left the house. Many of the shops had their shutters half down, and those that were open had no customers. Even the shopkeepers were asleep on the narrow strip of floor behind their counters, knowing that no one would care to come out in the mid-afternoon heat to steal sweets, bundles of bidis or a banana from the withered bunches that hung from hooks on the ceiling. The only person outside was an old woman sitting by an overflowing dustbin, feeding her cow a half-rotted jackfruit. She didn't even look at Sudha and me, not even when a street dog lying in the strip of shade created by a parapet began to bark at us, then raised its head in a long mournful howl.

'That's what they do when they see the devil,' I remembered.

I looked up at Sudha nervously. She hadn't said a word to me since we left the house. She walked purposefully and very fast, looking for something in particular. She stopped before a sweet shop. It was the least tempting of any sweet shop I had ever seen. Even Kodai might have been put off by it. The glass panes on the counter were brown with a pale layer of grease, and there seemed nothing to buy except two slabs of a sticky something, as yellow as adulterated turmeric. But I could smell something else cooking, so there must have been someone in the kitchen behind the shop.

Sudha wanted to go up to the second floor, where a black and white sign said simply 'Clinic' in both Tamil and English.

'Where are the stairs?' I heard her ask herself. They were built into a secret little hole by the sweet shop, and as I followed Sudha I wondered how old the building was and whether the staircase would collapse under our weight in a tremendous mushroom cloud of rubble and dust.

Even at that time I knew that everyone, especially my own parents, would disapprove of this expedition, more than of anything else Sudha had done or would do later on. 'Why,' they would ask disapprovingly, 'did she have to drag a child into all that?'

But I thought I knew why. I climbed steadily up the narrow stairway with my skirt wrapped closely around my body, making certain that nothing but my feet touched the floor or the walls, both as sticky as fly-traps. The stairs were splattered with betel juice the colour of dried blood, and at the top there was a heap of dirty white cloth cut into strips.

*   *   *

I waited between the low narrow door Sudha was behind and the sign saying, 'Excel Medical Centre – Western and Native Treatment for Piles and STD'. Because of everything that happened after that, I forgot to check the meaning of 'STD' till much later back home when I came across it once again.

It was the doctor – if he was a doctor – who suggested I stay outside. He didn't look like a doctor should, I thought. He hadn't bothered to smile a pro-fessional doctor's smile at us. Sudha was calm and self-possessed and stood there before him with nothing on her face, neither fear nor remorse nor humiliation. It was almost as if she had done this before. Only when she whispered that I had better go out, and I – never so glad to leave a room in which grown-ups were going to have what was sure to be an interesting conversation – turned to the door, she said, 'But you will *stay*, won't you?' And I knew that she was begging me to wait outside, not to run home.

'I will,' I promised. I stumbled onto the balcony.

For the first time I was frightened. I now knew why Sudha had come. What if she died in there while I stood outside and looked down at that empty street? Maybe I should have insisted on staying inside with her, I thought half-heartedly, but the sharp smell of medicine and something else inside had made me dizzy, made me want to get out, run down the stairs and get home. The smell of oil, sugar syrup and milk floated up from the sweet shop as I waited. They were making something fried and very syrupy – gulab jamun, maybe. I wanted to lean against the rickety balcony and vomit quietly, letting it all slide down the dirty, peeling walls of this ugly building.

When Sudha opened the door and came out I didn't look in to see what the man was doing.

'Let's go,' she said, and I followed her. It was not till we were out in the street that I asked her what the doctor had said.

She looked at me, not seeming to care that I knew why she had come here. 'He says he can't do it for such little money.'

He hadn't looked capable of being mean, but I could believe anything now.

'How much do you have with you?' I asked.

'Three hundred rupees.'

'Is there no way you can get more?'

'How can I?'

It was four o'clock. The shops were opening and the streets were getting more crowded. We couldn't find a cycle or auto-rickshaw quickly. I would have liked to have stood somewhere with a little shade and waited for one to come, but Sudha wanted to walk.

'Come on,' she said, and tugged at my elbow. As if walking on and on and on would help. Someone looking down from far above at that moment would have seen a mesh of narrow streets sizzling in the heat, and the two of us hurrying through it. Sudha, a tiny little insect whose wings had been singed, and me, too exhausted to think or feel anything. All I wanted was a cool, hard surface – the white door of a fridge, or a translucent block of dripping ice, or the pale-blue wall of an air-conditioned room, to lean my sweaty forehead against. But when we did manage to get a rickshaw and asked to be taken all the way home rather than just to the bus stand, I asked her if she knew anyone else who could do it for less.

'You should find out,' I urged, trying to sound encouraging.

She didn't reply. Then she said, 'There are other ways to do it. Other kinds of people who can also manage these things.'

'And you think there are people like that here?'

'There must be. They are everywhere.'

'Let's look for them then.' I pictured witches, mid-wives, crazy old men with wild eyes and magic spells. Though I really only wanted to get home.

'I'm frightened,' she said, looking down at the rick-shaw floor, which was so rusty that a small portion of it had worn away and we could see the road below us. 'You can even die at the end of it.'

So she was afraid to die even then. When we got off, though, a couple of streets from our own, she didn't look the least bit nervous. Only her hair was beginning to look uncombed, and she smelled very slightly of sweat. I saw that the back of her blouse was soaked and there were damp yellow stains under her arms. Her eyes were wide and dark. Her lips moved silently.

'She *has* gone mad now,' I decided. But when she spoke to me it was only to say that she would have another talk with Sundar and find someone the very next day to take her place.

When we got home and into the front room Janaki was coming in through the back door.

'Where have you been?' she asked Sudha. 'Lakshmi needs to be milked.'

'I'll do it now.' Sudha spoke as calmly as Janaki had done.

Janaki turned to me. 'And where did you go without telling anyone?'

'I left a note for you, didn't I?' I said sullenly.

'Yes, but I didn't know where you had gone.'

'Were you worried?'

She didn't reply.

'We decided to go to the temple,' I said coldly, defying her to ask me anything more.

The clock struck five. Our trip had lasted nearly four hours. Sudha finished with Lakshmi and went upstairs; it was Janaki who cooked dinner. I went out to the bathroom to wash away the grime and terror of our expedition. When I got back Janaki was no longer in the kitchen or upstairs in her room. I went to Sudha's room and saw both of them there. Sudha was standing against the wall, and Janaki stood stiff and upright as though everything in there – the walls, the mirror, the mattress – were unclean.

'You should go home,' she was telling Sudha.

I slipped in and stood at the door.

'That's the only thing for you to do now – go home.'

'You know I can't go home,' Sudha said.

'I can't think of what else you can do, then,' Janaki said coldly.

'Don't you think your brother should do something – about all this?' Sudha asked.

Janaki shrugged. 'From what you tell me, it looks like he's decided not to.'

I shifted, and Janaki turned around and saw me.

'Please go downstairs, Nithya.'

'No.'

'You must,' she said, her voice as cold as when she was talking to Sudha. She had never spoken to me like that before. I left the room and she came with me right to the top of the stairs and watched till I had got halfway down them before she turned to go back to Sudha's room. I waited on the last step for a minute before running quietly back upstairs. This time I stood outside the door and listened, as I had listened to Sundar and Sudha outside the kitchen.

'Where did you go this afternoon, taking Nithya with you?' Janaki asked.

For a moment I thought Sudha would tell her. I could see her expression change from anger to guilt and fear. But all she said was, 'Why don't you ask her yourself?'

'I told you to keep away from that child. That's what my sister would want. You have taught her to lie and to hide things from us – just like you do.' Janaki turned away as if she had finished, and I got ready to run back downstairs.

'You've never liked me,' Sudha said very softly, and she sat down on her bed, 'because I'm different from you. I have things you'll never have. You can't bear to see anyone happy . . . you want us all to be as lonely as you.'

Janaki had her back to me, but suddenly she did seem lonely as she stood there listening to Sudha. I saw her pull her sari close around her shoulders.

'Even now, in spite of everything that's happened, I'm grateful that I am not you,' Sudha continued. And Janaki stepped back.

My heart thumped so loudly that I wondered how they could fail to hear it, and my legs felt weak beneath me. They were both silent.

'You came here to spoil everything I had,' Janaki said. 'I never wanted you to come. I didn't want anyone else here. It was he who insisted.'

'What *did* you have?' Sudha asked fiercely. 'Even Sundar has you in his house only because he has to.'

'I had – peace. Sometimes,' Janaki said. 'Why don't you go to Madras? You can have your child or get rid of it – it doesn't matter what you do. And there is plenty a woman like you can do to make money there.'

'Maybe I *will* go to Madras,' Sudha said slowly, as if she just realized that the idea made sense.

'You are a disgrace to everything,' Janaki continued as though she couldn't stop herself. 'To your people, to your caste, especially to your poor parents.'

Sudha turned pale. She had nothing to say to that.

'If I were you I'd want to be dead,' Janaki hissed. 'I'd kill myself, that's what I would do. Why don't you do that?'

A long black snake, as slender as a worm, slithered

across the floor and raised its little head. Sudha stared at it in fascination.

'Maybe I will,' she said for the second time.

The sudden sound of music startled all of us. They had turned on the microphone at the Hanuman temple again, and the sound of the chanting that Sridhar had objected to earlier rumbled across the streets, through the trees and into the room. Janaki turned and left. When she passed me I could almost hear her fast, shallow breathing. She looked straight ahead and didn't see me.

I stopped to see what Sudha was doing before I followed Janaki. She stood up calmly and I thought that she, too, was going to leave her room. I went downstairs. Janaki was outside, splashing water over her face and rinsing her mouth out, as if it were dirty.

*   *   *

I never found out whether anything else happened that day. Sundar came home much later than usual and Sudha didn't come down from her room. I decided to lie down till it was time for me to eat, and drifted off to sleep. Though I didn't ask the next morning, I didn't think anyone tried to wake me up – they had too much on their minds that night. I woke up the next morning and realized I had slept for a very long time and would never know whether Sudha had spoken to Sundar again.

When I came down I saw that someone had left coffee out for me. It had turned cold and I poured it into the backyard, a long brown coffee waterfall splattering off the hibiscus leaves. Sundar must have left for work. Janaki was sweeping the house. Sudha was still in her room, and I wondered if she had come down at all. I stayed in the kitchen.

At eleven o'clock, when I decided to have a bath and went up to get my clothes, I saw that Janaki was also in her room, reading the newspaper.

It was very hot outside. The next day's papers said it was the hottest day of the year. After I had my bath and dried myself, I felt fine beads of sweat break out on my back and arms. When I came out I found a baby crow lying beneath the mango tree, dazed by the heat. I reached out, but it croaked and flew clumsily up to perch on the lowest branch.

I didn't want to go upstairs and sit with Janaki so I stayed in the front room. At one o'clock I heard Sundar's scooter and looked out the window, wondering why he had come home at that time of day. He left the scooter out by the gate and I opened the door without waiting for him to knock. He didn't even look at me, just went out to the garden and straight into the bathroom. I went out to wait for him in the garden but it was so hot that I came back inside. The house was almost as dark as night after the light outside, and I had to wait for my eyes to adjust before I went upstairs and found Sudha dead.

Chapter Eight

Few of those who came to look at Sudha, and had been in and out of Sundar's house since the evening after her death, returned straight home after the funeral. I saw Seshadri cross the street and knock at Gopal's door, and even Narayan Mama, striding homeward with umbrella unfurled, turned around when someone called out to him. Kodai told me later that it had been a while since there had been a marriage or death on GC Street, and now there was an unexpected death, a suicide – and in Sundar and Janaki's household, where nothing had happened for years.

Some of the excitement communicated itself to the children. It made them want to run out into the street and play. I had rarely seen children come outside in this neighbourhood; they usually kept to their gardens.

A dozen little girls stood in two rows several feet apart, facing each other.

'*Varugirom, varugirom, indha maadhathil . . .*'

They strung their arms around each other's waists

and rocked and swayed forward. Their voices were high and clear.

'*Yendha poove parika varigire, varigire indha maadhathil . . .*'

Which flower are you coming to pick, coming to pick, coming to pick . . .

Which flower are you coming to pick this season?

'*Malli poove parika varugirom . . .*'

We're going to pick the jasmine . . . or the rose . . . or the champak . . . and the girl who was the jasmine or the rose or the champak would come timidly to the middle to be picked and would spin around, her arms stretched out before her, then drop to the ground in a heap of wilting petals.

Sundar and Janaki didn't come down and I didn't want to go upstairs. I crouched by the window sill and looked out into the street over the low wall, hoping no one would notice me. Even if I had wanted to, it just wouldn't do for me to join the other children just then. I didn't expect to see Kodai out playing with the others so I wasn't surprised that she wasn't there. I waited for the priest at the Hanuman temple to ring the bells. When he did, at precisely six o'clock, people slowly began drifting out of each other's houses, and after lingering at front doors and gates a little while longer, they went home. Some stopped to take their children back home, scolding them in hushed voices or twisting their ears all the way to their doorsteps. And suddenly there was nothing for me to look at.

When I went into the kitchen I could find only a single overripe banana to eat. Someone knocked on the door and before I could get to it Janaki came downstairs and answered it. It was Narayan Mama's daughter-in-law Vaishnavi.

'We wondered if you'd need some food for tonight. We could pack something for you and send it over . . .' She peered over Janaki's shoulder into the front room.

'No,' Janaki said, 'we have cooked for the night.'

She had opened the door only partially, and she stood firmly before it as though Vaishnavi might actually force her way inside. Janaki waited for her to leave.

'Are you sure?' Vaishnavi persisted. 'My father-in-law would be very upset if you both had nothing to eat tonight.'

'I'm sure,' Janaki said. She was very tired.

'Sulochana was also wondering if she should come over and ask if you need anything.'

'Do me a favour, Vaishnavi,' Janaki said. 'Stop at Sulochana's house on your way back and tell her not to worry about us. We don't need anything tonight. We have decided to go to sleep early.'

Vaishnavi left, and Janaki shut the door and drew the latch. She went into the kitchen and I went back to my post at the window.

A bicycle stopped at our gate soon after that, and a man in khaki uniform got off. I thought it was another policeman but the battered bag slung over his shoulder told me it was the man who delivered telegrams. He knocked on the door and I had jumped up and gone to open it when I felt Janaki's hand on my shoulder holding me back.

'Let it be,' she murmured.

'But it's a telegram,' I whispered back fiercely.

'I know. Let it be.'

He knocked again. And again, for a third time, before he left.

'It might have been from my parents,' I said accusingly, making my voice deliberately loud.

'Probably not. Sundar hasn't yet written to them. He will do it tomorrow morning. They'd have no reason to send us a telegram now.'

'But it might be something else – something important.'

'He'll bring it back tomorrow.'

He did return the next day with a telegram from Sudha's uncle, her father's brother. He had supposed that Sudha's father would still be at Sundar's house and had telegraphed to ask if he wanted someone else to join him at Thiruninravur. I never found out whether Sundar forwarded the telegram to Sudha's village.

But that was the next day. No one else came to the door that second evening after Sudha died. It was already dark when I heard Lakshmi moo loudly.

'Maybe she's not feeling well,' I thought, and before I could decide whether to fetch Janaki or Sundar, Sundar came down himself.

'Something is wrong with Lakshmi,' I told him.

'Nothing is wrong with her. It's just that she hasn't been milked.'

And he went into the backyard and returned in a while with the milk. I hadn't known that Sundar could milk cows.

After he went back to his room I slipped out to see Lakshmi, stopping to light a kerosene lamp because I didn't want to switch on the light over the door and attract Kodai's or her mother's attention. The lamp was a rusty one. Anyone looking out at the garden would barely have seen the faint light bobbing and dipping among the trees and rustling shadows. Lakshmi was drinking thirstily out of the trough of fresh water Sundar had filled for her. She looked enormous as she stood there in the dull light of my lamp. I went right into the shed and reached out to touch her side as Sudha had urged me many times to do.

'There's no reason to be frightened of a *buffalo*!' she would say, laughing. 'What do you think – a buffalo is a *wild* animal?'

Lakshmi's skin was rough, and her short bristly hair prickled against my palm. She didn't even seem to feel my hand on her, or in any case think it worth her while to stop drinking.

'Will you eat now?' Janaki asked when I went back indoors.

'I don't want to eat,' I said, and she didn't try to persuade me. She and Sundar didn't seem to want to eat, either. Janaki shut the back door and went back upstairs. The two vessels of food she had just cooked stayed out the whole night and turned stale by the morning.

I decided to stay up that night. I lay down on my mattress and waited. Janaki went to sleep unusually quickly. I listened to her soft, regular breathing for a while and then left the room, carrying my pillow and sheet with me. I could see a strip of light under Sundar's door but I knew he wouldn't come downstairs. And if Janaki woke up later and came looking for me I could always say I had found it too hot upstairs.

I leant against the wall of the front room, wrapped

my sheet around me and waited. I remembered how dark and still the nights had seemed when I first got here and how quickly I had got used to them and I wondered if the hum of the traffic and the blue-whiteness of fluorescent street lamps would bother me when I went back home.

Nothing happened. The clock on the wall whirred and grumbled softly before striking one o'clock. The murmur of the ceiling fan was interrupted every few seconds by a little click. It didn't seem to get any cooler at night in this house. I threw off my sheet impatiently and wondered how much longer it would be before the sun rose. Some people on the street, Ambuja Pati for instance, would be up in a couple of hours, and between five and six o'clock Sundar and Janaki would come down. I woke up when the clock struck two and stumbled upstairs, my eyes barely open, the sheet trailing up the steps behind me like a ghostly mantle.

*   *   *

'Are you not going to the office today?' I heard Janaki ask Sundar the next morning.

He had not changed his clothes, and had taken his coffee and morning meal in his veshti and under-shirt.

'No.'

She hesitated before asking him why. Still, it was the first time I had heard her question any of Sundar's decisions.

'Because I don't feel like it,' he said. He got up to wash his hands.

'Are you going to Aathur to look at the land?'

'No. I'll stay home today,' he said, and went out into the garden.

I didn't exactly feel unwell when I went up to Sudha's room that morning. I only had a headache, though I had refused to eat that morning.

'You didn't have any dinner last night, either,' Janaki had reminded me.

'I know.' But my stomach had still turned at the thought of any food.

Someone had bolted Sudha's door from outside. I pushed it open hoping neither Sundar nor Janaki would hear. Nothing had been disturbed inside. Only the police constable had drawn a circle with yellow chalk on the ceiling where the body had hung and a circle around the corresponding point on the floor. The windows had been pulled shut. Sudha had never shut them, had not even shut them before she died. The room was so still and dark that it could be night in there. My head was beginning to ache badly and I shivered. I was not feeling well, and knew I should leave this room and go to bed. But the policemen had not looked at the floor carefully enough. I saw a strand of hair and bent to pick it up. Sudha's. And suddenly the sound of her name screeched and roared in my ears and a hundred sneering faces circled around me. I was trapped at the centre of a demonic merry-go-round. I sat on the floor and buried my head between my knees to make the dizziness go away.

'What are you doing in here, Nithya?'

I hadn't even heard Janaki come in. I looked up and saw that her face was pale and sad and cunning.

'You shouldn't be in this room,' she said, and she came softly towards me.

'Leave me alone!' I screamed. And I tried to stand up but the room was dark and my legs were no longer mine.

The well in Sundar's backyard was the deepest darkest well in the world.

'It leads to Hell!' Kodai was shouting in both my ears. 'It leads to Hell. That's what my brother says and he knows everything.'

So I sat on the rim and swung my legs into the well. My legs were long and thin, as if they were made of elastic, and I felt the cool blast of air from the bottom hit the soles of my feet.

'Do you want to get inside?' someone asked me from behind. I tried to place the voice – Sundar or Janaki or Sudha. Kodai or Sridhar. And whoever it was pushed me in. I whirled through the darkness kicking and waving my arms and legs in a mad dance, not afraid of what I would find at the bottom but frightened that the damp mossy walls would close in and trap me between them for ever. I hit water and gasped as I sank and rose and sank again.

'What do you think is the matter with her?' Janaki was asking Sundar.

I was now in her room, and they were both standing over me as if I were another dead body. I struggled to get up and run out of the room but another wave of nausea hit me. I retched and saw food I had never eaten fall onto the pillow. My head turned, and it was an effort to keep myself from falling face down in the mess.

'If she goes on like this we'll have to get a doctor,' Sundar said, reaching down to touch my forehead. 'She has a fever. A high fever.'

And he held my head up while Janaki changed the pillow cover. I had always hated him, and now I hated his touch and nearness and smell, but was too weak to protest. They put a blanket over me and left the room.

I woke up in a sweat and kicked the blankets off but soon shivered and pulled them on again. It was difficult to say what time it was. I looked outside – the sky was a dull angry red. My skin was burning and there was a thud in my ears like someone was drumming persistently very, very far away or deep inside my head. There was also a smell in the room. It wasn't just the smell of my vomit and sweat, it was the combined stink of filthy air, dirty water and congested drains, the hot blood of animals splashed on the pavement outside a slaughterhouse I had once walked past, and the sourness of the pillows. I tried to hold my breath but had to let go in a few minutes and the smell rushed into my nostrils and mouth and stomach with a small gurgle. It wasn't just this room – the house was smelling, and the compound and the other houses and streets beyond. They would have to do something about this quickly.

Some people were talking in low voices. There were two of them and now more than two, a big crowd of them and then the first two again, pretending to be two other people.

'Yes, she was very ill . . . maybe she shouldn't stay here in this house any more . . . and she hasn't eaten properly for two days . . . What was she doing in that room this morning anyway . . . she shouldn't have been allowed in there . . .'

I waited for them to say Sudha's name, but they

avoided it carefully as if it would burn their mouths or set the air around them on fire.

Someone placed a cool clean hand on my forehead and I struggled to open my eyes.

'Don't worry, it's only Dr Raghavan,' Sundar said in a gentle voice that was not Sundar's. I shut my eyes again and let the voices in my head rise to a hysterical crescendo. I knew that that other doctor, who wasn't really a doctor at all, had found his way into the house to do to me whatever he could have done to Sudha or to tell Sundar and Janaki what had been Sudha's secret from everyone in the world but me. I tried to sit up because I had to stop him from talking but someone pushed me back onto the pillow. He was gentle but I hit out at him and clawed at his face.

'She is certainly very ill . . .' The little insect-voices had begun their murmur again. 'She has high fever . . . nervous tension . . . you know all this is not good for a child, Sundar.'

'Yes,' I said, surfacing for a minute out of the mist that surrounded me. 'It's all too confusing, too much.' I wanted to go home.

Sundar and Janaki were with me, and a bearded stranger who sat on the edge of my bed and smiled at me kindly.

'You will be fine soon,' he said. 'I've left some medicines with your uncle.' He turned to Sundar and Janaki. 'Don't let her sleep by herself tonight.'

'No, she always sleeps with my sister,' Sundar said.

The light was making my eyes burn. 'No!' I choked over a sob. 'I don't want to sleep here.' Janaki's face changed. 'I don't want to stay here. I'm frightened,' I said. I tried to stand up but fell back onto the sheets and burst into tears.

'Poor child. The last few days have really been difficult for her.' The doctor was sitting by my side again. Through my tears I saw Sundar and Janaki standing behind him like two uneasy ghosts.

I floated in and out of my fever for two whole days. The house was very, very still except when the doctor came in a second time, and was also unbelievably cold. I shook beneath the two blankets Janaki had got out for me and my head ached and spun so violently that I had to push it under my pillow to still it. Janaki was in the room a lot of the time – I would see her sitting on her bed with her books or newspaper or stitching work and would turn my face away to the wall and shut my eyes and pretend to be asleep.

One afternoon when I woke up and saw that she was not there, I got out of bed and went out of the room. I stopped at the top of the stairs. The steps had turned gigantic and flowed into each other like low, rounded hillocks. If I climbed down them they would heave me up to the ceiling in one huge noiseless movement. But I couldn't get myself to go back to those three bedrooms with the doors that were nearly always shut. I was trapped in this house and my parents would never come to get me. The thought filled me with dread. I knew then that Sudha too had been this frightened only four days ago and had twisted her sari into a rope. The world began spinning around me again. I staggered back to the room and fell into bed.

When I got up I started a letter to my mother. 'Dear Amma and Daddy,' I wrote in the third of the six aerogrammes, 'I'm frightened . . . come and take me

177

back home. I can't sleep at night any more. I want to go home.'

I pushed the unfinished letter under my pillow and tried to sleep.

When I woke up that night the house was warm for the first time in three days. I turned to look at Janaki on her bed and thought of that night long, long ago when I had woken up and seen her standing before her mirror. At that time it had made me wonder, but I thought I understood a little better now. The clock downstairs struck as it had during my nighttime vigil three nights ago, which seemed so meaningless now.

'I'll never know why I do the things I sometimes do,' I thought. I lay still, my eyes wide open.

'Dear God, let everything be all right,' I then blabbered softly. 'Let Sudha be all right now and Amma and Daddy. And Janaki. Let it not be so hot let the next two months pass quickly maybe it will rain tomorrow because it has to rain *sometime* and the street would be a stretch of swampy mud where the children could splash their way home and the wet air would be heavy with those insects whose names Amma has told me many times, which come out only after the rain . . .'

* * *

When I looked at myself in the mirror the next day I saw that my skin had turned dark, as if I had been out in the sun, and my eyes had sunk deep into my face. I looked down at my arms – they seemed thin and feeble, and the fine hair that grew on them, which I had never been aware of till a few months ago, was suddenly darker and thicker and more visible. I hadn't brushed my teeth for two days and hadn't had a bath. I hated my own body, and tried not to let my tongue touch the surface of my teeth. But I didn't want to leave the room – not just yet. I went back to bed and lay down and closed my eyes. But I couldn't fall asleep. It was bright outside and the mattress was unpleasantly warm beneath me. I couldn't believe I had actually been feeling cold till yesterday and had used two blankets. I was also getting very hungry – I would have to go downstairs soon. Janaki came in.

'Are you feeling better?'

'I'm fine,' I said.

'You've been very ill – you know that?'

'I know.'

I was very still when she placed a cool hand on my forehead.

'You don't seem to have fever, but you'd better wear this.'

She gave me a sweater. It was too large for me and smelt musty – no one ever had to wear sweaters in Thiruninravur – and was moth-eaten at the collar and elbows. I started to protest but decided not to. But when I got to the bottom of the stairs I was sweating so much that I took it off and threw it across the room. I had reached the kitchen door when I turned back and picked it up impatiently. I bundled it up under my arm and went into the kitchen.

'You are up today?'

I was surprised by the relief in Sundar's voice. He actually seemed glad that I was downstairs once more.

The coffee tasted bitter and I asked for milk instead. Janaki poured it for me and they both watched me drink. I was both pleased and discomfited by this

179

sudden demonstration of concern. It made them both seem like strangers. Sundar even smiled at me as he wheeled his scooter out. It didn't occur to me until later that Janaki had not seen him off at the door.

She let me have a bath that day but insisted on heating the water in the garden in a vessel as big and black as a witch's cauldron. It didn't look like it had been used for years – its bottom was covered with a layer of twigs and dry leaves, and when we picked it up a skinny little brown spider dashed frantically around the inside. The hot water, when it was ready, smelt of wood smoke and I poured some of it over my head. I wanted my hair to smell like that, too.

This upset Janaki. 'You shouldn't have washed your hair today. You've been ill – it would have been better if you'd waited a while.'

'But I didn't wash my hair – I just poured some water over my head – just one vessel.'

'But it makes sense for you to keep your scalp dry just now.'

The afternoon passed in a dull, peaceful haze. Janaki only gave me a very watery rice porridge, which I ate with a spoon. I decided to ask for something more after that – spicy vegetables, rice loaded with ghee, fiery pickle. But when I finished the last spoonful I found that I was full and very slightly ill.

When I woke up that evening I realized I had slept for quite a while. Janaki was downstairs. She would have to spend more time in the kitchen and backyard now because there was no one to help her around the house. It was dull up here. I jumped up, wandered downstairs, came up again, threw myself on the bed and almost wished I were ill again.

After making me take two spoonfuls of a strange-smelling brown tonic, Janaki let me go into the backyard. I wandered among the trees, touching their barks and feeling their leaves. They were old friends. Janaki had asked me to put on the blue cap I was carrying, and I had agreed because the sun's light still made my eyes water. But after I had been around the backyard twice and around to the front of the house once, there was nothing left to do. I had already been into Sundar's room that morning. There had been nothing new there, either.

I was almost glad to see Kamala come into her backyard and begin to take clothes off the line. I went towards the hibiscus bushes and stood there. I didn't have to wait long – she pulled the last sari off the line and her eyes wandered to Sundar's house. Her face lit up when she saw me.

'Oh, Nithya!' She covered the distance between her clothesline and the bushes very quickly for someone so heavy, her face half covered by the bundle of clothes in her arms.

'And how are you feeling now? We heard you have been ill.' She impatiently pushed down with her chin a starched shirt that was blocking her view. 'Do you know I haven't seen anyone from your house since – that day? Hasn't Sundar been going to the office?'

'No, he's been at home.' At once I regretted having said that. I didn't mean to tell any of them anything.

'Yes, that's what we thought. But I can understand why . . . so many problems . . . and all because of that girl.'

I wanted to go in but thought of the long evening stretching before me and decided to stay on.

'But tell me about yourself. Didn't Dr Raghavan visit you two times? He would only tell us that you had fever. Was that all that actually happened?'

'It was just that. I had a fever.'

'Oh, you poor thing. Such a bad time for you to be in that house. You must be feeling terrible.' I believe she would have reached across and smothered me in her arms if it hadn't been for the clothes.

'Do you want to come and stay with us for some days?' she offered. 'We could talk to Sundar about it.'

I shook my head.

'Think about it,' Kamala went on eagerly. 'You can come here any time you like. You'll have Kodai to keep you company all day.' She smiled eagerly. 'In fact, why don't you come in for a few minutes right now? Everyone is at home except my husband.'

I trailed behind her across their garden and into their house. I had been there several times but still looked around carefully to see if anything had changed. I knew that something must have changed somewhere after all that had happened. It was not possible for things to go on just as they had done before. But Kamala's large, smoky kitchen was just as it had always been – not as neat as Janaki's, with stray bits of vegetable peels on the floor and stains on the walls and the kerosene stove. Kamala smelt like her kitchen, too, smelt of oil, red chilli powder and turmeric. Ambuja Pati was in the front room and Kodai was probably inside. She kept away from her grandmother as often as she could because Ambuja Pati was always scolding her – Kodai ate too much, she slept at odd hours, she didn't like having a bath early in the day and, according to Ambuja Pati, she was sly and smirked and grinned behind her elders' backs. The old lady had no patience with Sridhar, either, even though everyone knew that he was clever, one of the best students in his class at college.

She was sitting in her corner when I came in, her eyes closed, praying under her breath.

'Sit down here,' Kamala whispered. 'I'll get you some buttermilk. You are allowed to drink that, aren't you? Buttermilk is good at any time.'

'Yes. And anyway I'm not ill any more.'

Though I sat down in the corner of the room farthest from Ambuja Pati, I could see that the crevices on her face and arms had folded into a thousand creases. The flesh between every deep fold was grey, as if some species of dusty fungus grew there. Even her eyelids were wrinkled, and her thick eyebrows were white beneath the white sari.

'*Om Namo Vishnava Prabhavishnave . . .*' I heard her mutter angrily. And then she opened her eyes.

Kamala came in just then with the buttermilk. 'So you've finished praying, Amma,' she said in the conciliating tone I always heard her use with her mother-in-law. 'Nithya is here.'

'I can see that.'

Kodai came out and sat on the chair. I sipped the buttermilk and wondered what I was doing with these three people who never failed to irritate me.

Sridhar came down the stairs. He looked as if he had been ill himself, or was very tired. He glanced at me and went back upstairs without saying a word. Kodai got up as if she wanted to follow her brother, but changed her mind and settled herself again on the chair.

'Why are you wearing a topi on your head?' Kodai leaned forward and asked me, holding one plump cheek in her hand as if she had a toothache.

'Kodai has a toothache,' Kamala whispered to me. 'Only don't mention it before Ambuja Pati. She'll say the poor child eats too many sweets.'

I barely heard Kamala. I quickly snatched off my cap and said, 'Because it's hot outside. That's why. Why else would anyone want to wear a cap?'

'But you are not outside any more,' Kodai pointed out.

I was angry with myself for giving Kodai a chance to make me feel ridiculous.

'Oh, how much you children argue!' Kamala laughed.

'Come closer, child,' Ambuja Pati ordered me.

I thought of getting up and leaving, saying that I had to get home, but I left my empty buttermilk glass on the floor and went and sat closer to Ambuja Pati.

'So all kinds of things have been happening at Sundar's house?' Ambuja Pati said.

What does she expect me to say to that? I wondered. I stared straight back into the stern grey eyes.

'I am not interested in the girl who killed herself. Everyone knows what happened to her – a girl with neither sense or good conduct, she deserved all that she got,' Ambuja Pati said.

'Yes,' Kamala sighed, 'but we are not even sure if she was really pregnant . . .' She looked at Kodai and me and stopped.

'I never really thought she was that kind of girl, though,' Kamala continued. 'I'd see her busy in the garden every day, morning and evening, and I would sometimes call out to her and she'd chatter away to me like an innocent little child.'

I wondered if that was true. It probably was. Sudha had liked everyone in the world – the stupid, the irritating, the bad, she had never passed judgement on them and could be nice to them without having to try too hard. And the Sudha I had first met had also loved to talk.

Come on, Nithya, let's talk.

But I need to finish tracing out this map, I would sometimes say, or *finish my sums* or *read this by five o'clock*.

And will you come as soon as you finish?

Ambuja Pati went on as though *she* hadn't been interrupted by Kamala: 'What I want to know is about Janaki. How is she taking it? All this – rubbish – happening around her.'

'I don't know. You should ask her yourself,' I said. The two of them stared at me.

I looked at Kodai, wondering why *she* hadn't asked any questions yet. But she didn't even seem to be listening. She was plaiting together the strips of brightly coloured cotton she had on her lap.

'Ask Janaki to come and talk to me sometime,' Ambuja Pati said, and she hobbled back into her corner and shut her eyes.

Kamala was quiet for a few minutes, as though she expected her mother-in-law to speak again. When it was clear that Ambuja Pati didn't mean to, Kamala whispered to Kodai and me, 'Go and play upstairs. Or in the garden. Only don't make a noise.' As if either us us ever did.

We went up to sit with Sridhar. He had a room of

his own, with a bookshelf and a large desk, though most of it was taken up by stacks of shirts and undershirts that his mother had washed and folded but not put back into his cupboard. He was sitting at the desk doodling.

'Look, Anna, Nithya has a topi – like a boy.' Kodai pointed to the cap I now held in my hand. Sridhar looked at it without interest.

'Why didn't you ever talk to us about all those things happening in your house?' he asked me.

'What things?'

'About Sudha and Sundar.'

'Aren't you assuming things you don't know enough about?' I asked stiffly.

He seemed taken aback for a minute. 'But that's what the post-mortem report said, didn't it? That she might have been pregnant?'

'Well, it might have been wrong.'

Sridhar shrugged. 'Most people don't think so. And no one can think of who else it could be but Sundar. Even I'm a bit surprised at him, you know – in his own house, with you and especially Janaki living there. And Sudha being a brahmin girl, a priest's daughter.'

I stared at the two of them silently.

'Do you know why she killed herself?' Kodai had crept up to me and thrust her neck forward as if she were trying to mesmerize me into answering.

'Shut up, Kodai. *I'm* talking to Nithya,' Sridhar said irritably, and Kodai moved away sulkily. But she didn't leave the room. She crouched on the bed and waited for me to say something.

I felt a slow, new excitement prick at the back of my head. I suddenly saw how important all this was and how important I was to all these people – Sridhar, Kodai, Ambuja Pati, Kamala, Vasu, Narayan Mama and all the others on this street. Because I had actually been in the house when it happened.

'Was she very unhappy before she died?' Sridhar asked softly. I sensed he was not just being curious when he asked me that. But I was not going to answer any questions yet.

'I don't know,' I said.

'She must have been.' He sounded rather sad himself, and it occurred to me that he was much nicer than his mother and sister and almost everyone else around here.

'I always thought of her as something – something – ethereal . . . like a star maybe, or a ray of light.'

My momentary sympathy for him vanished. I found this irritating and stupid. A ray of light you wanted to see without its clothes on, I thought.

'It's strange. She looked as she always did, even over the last few weeks,' Sridhar said.

'So you've been spying on her!' I accused him.

Sridhar flushed. 'That's ridiculous. I just saw her one or two times in your garden or at your gate.'

I didn't say anything to that.

'Do you think she was very unhappy?' he asked again.

'Maybe she wasn't.'

They were puzzled by my reply. But I had had enough for now.

'I'm going home,' I announced, and I went out of the room. Neither of them bothered to follow me so I went down the stairs by myself.

'Rude things,' I thought. 'I'll never come here again or tell them any of the things they want to know.'

Kamala leapt up from the chair. 'Did you have a nice time with Sridhar and Kodai?' she asked. 'Why don't you stay for a little longer and talk to me in the kitchen?'

'No, I have to go home,' I said firmly. She looked disappointed,

'But you should come again. It will be a change for you. And you should spend more time playing with the children around here. It will do you good after – everything. Will you come again?' she asked anxiously.

'I will.'

*   *   *

There was a telegram from my parents waiting at home. *Shocked by the news stop very worried about Nithya stop does she want to change present arrangements stop Nithya and Sundar write back in detail stop*.

Sundar must have telegraphed them, if they had learnt what had happened so quickly.

'Dear Amma and Daddy,' I began the fourth of my letters. I thought for a minute. 'Don't worry about me. It's all over now and I am fine. I've even managed to get quite a bit of schoolwork done so there is no need for you to be anxious about that. And please don't think there should be any change in the arrangements you've made for me. It's only another two months anyway. How is Daddy's project going and how . . .'

I finished and sealed the letter and went out to post it in the box I had discovered down the street. I was back in ten minutes and I looked for the other letter I had started when I was ill. When I found it I tore it up carefully before I threw it away.

Chapter Nine

Janaki later asked me where I'd been after lunch.

'I went to see Kodai,' I said.

She must have found that strange. She knew I didn't like visiting Kodai.

There was plenty for Janaki to do around the house now. She even let me help her more often than she used to before. I cleaned the kitchen floor after every meal and she even let me sweep the house sometimes. Raju, the milkman, who had come in once before when Sudha was away visiting her parents, began coming in again to milk and clean Lakshmi.

'You must have seen the telegram from your parents,' Janaki said to me.

I nodded.

'They are worried about you.'

'I know.'

'They are wondering if you would like to go somewhere else for the next few weeks. I think Sundar, too, feels you might be happier away from here.'

'What do *you* think? Do you think I should go away?' I asked.

'You should do whatever you want to do. I don't want you to be unhappy or frightened,' she said.

She struck her match and bent low over the kerosene stove to light it. The flame jumped up with a little pop and gasp and lit the lower part of her face, making her mouth look like it was on fire. When she turned away from it, her face was only half visible in the dark kitchen.

'I have to write to your mother soon. What should I tell her?'

'Tell her I'll stay. I'm not unhappy – or frightened,' I said.

I thought she was pleased at that, though she only nodded and said, 'I'll write to them this afternoon and tell them that, then.'

Janaki had changed. I could sense it – even though I didn't think I knew her really well even after all this while. I hadn't felt that way about Sudha though *she* had been the one thinking and doing things I knew very little about. And Janaki didn't ever talk like Amma liked to do – about her hopes and worries about me, my father, her plans for the next year, the year after and the next day's lunch. With Janaki I had to watch and wonder and wait. And because I watched so closely I knew that she had changed. She didn't look very different, nor did she say much more. But her shoulders didn't slump as they sometimes used to do, as if the weight of her long hair was too much for them to bear. And there was a restlessness in her that I had noticed sometimes before, only she no longer battled with it. She too was waiting for something to happen.

She waited patiently, going about her household work with a new-found authority. When Janaki had come out of Sudha's room the day before Sudha died, she'd still been uncertain. Perhaps she was now beginning to see Sudha's death as a triumph, a mark even of her ability to influence things.

I often thought about why Sudha had killed herself. She had meant to get things done the next day, that's what she had told me. I didn't know what that exchange with Janaki had done to her, or whether she had had another conversation with Sundar that had ended much like the one I had overheard and had given up, decided it was all too much for her. Death might have seemed simple and uncomplicated, like sleep.

But I also knew that I would never really know. I only knew that Janaki changed after Sudha died. Nearly every morning I watched her move silently around the kitchen, into the backyard and back into the house, up and down the stairs and I was fascinated and frightened.

Even Sundar must have sensed something different in her. He was uncomfortable in its presence. 'Don't bother about me from tomorrow. I'll serve myself when I eat,' he said one day when he was getting up to wash his hands. She listened to him, her face expressionless. That night she served him his food again, stood over him and watched every mouthful he swallowed. He began to look uneasy at every meal, indeed whenever he came downstairs.

One day I was up in Janaki's room when I heard his scooter draw up at the gate. After he had eaten he stopped to talk to me on the way to his room. He

191

hesitated and then came to stand in the doorway. I wondered why he didn't walk right in.

'How are you feeling today, Nithya?' he asked me.

'I'm all right.'

He turned away, then turned back and said, 'Janaki has told me that you have decided to stay on here till your amma and appa come back. Is that right?'

'Yes.'

'You have made up your mind about it, then.'

'Yes I have.'

'If you are so sure, I suppose I can write to them.'

'Janaki's already written,' I replied. I thought he was surprised at that, but he didn't say anything more. He went on to his room.

'Don't worry about me,' I called out after him, 'I'm not frightened.'

*　　*　　*

That afternoon Sridhar jumped over the bushes and came to watch me wash my clothes. Janaki was busy and didn't know about it or she wouldn't have allowed it. But I thought it would be fun to draw water from the well and watch the blue and pink soap bubbles settle on the washing stone and waft gently away when I blew at them.

'So you wash your own clothes now?' Sridhar asked.

'Only sometimes.'

'And Janaki does all the housework?'

'I didn't know you were interested in these things,' I said impatiently.

Sridhar flushed. 'I'm not. You have no idea how little I care about – anything,' he said gloomily. 'I'm going away, you know, as soon as I get my final exam results this June.' He had lowered his voice.

'Where are you going?'

'I don't know yet. To Madras, maybe. Or Trichi.'

'Are you going to become a priest – a Christian father?' I found the idea interesting.

'No, no. Whatever makes you think that? I'm just – going away. I need to get away from everything here.'

Before I could ask him anything else he wandered away across the backyard and out into the road behind, untroubled by the heat. I continued washing.

But that very evening Kodai peered into the backyard and signalled for me to come over. 'My brother asked me to call you. He wants to show you something.' I followed her up to Sridhar's room. Kamala didn't seem to be around, though I caught a glimpse of Ambuja Pati, a heap of white cloth crumpled in her corner. Sridhar was cutting something out of a newspaper with a pair of scissors.

'Oh, you've come!' he said. 'Give me a minute.' He had one clipping beside him already. When he finished cutting out the second one he looked for a pen, wrote something on both of them and handed them over to me.

'What are these?' I asked.

The clippings were over a week old. He had labelled them *The Hindu – April 18th 1986* and *Surya Kanthi, April 18th 1986*. The second one was a Tamil newspaper. I read the report from the *Hindu*.

'Thiruvallavur District, April 17th. A twenty-year-old girl allegedly committed suicide by hanging herself yesterday afternoon. The girl has been identified as Sudha of Thirukullam village. She was living with her relative S. Sundararajan and his family. Police are conducting investigations.'

That was all. One paragraph under 'District News'. But it mattered more than anything else anywhere in the world.

'Are they really conducting investigations?' I asked Sridhar.

'Of course they are. They have to. It is a case of unnatural death. Do you see what it says?' He pointed to the report. ' "A girl *allegedly* committed suicide." Do you know what *allegedly* means?'

'Of course I do,' I said scornfully.

He was excited. 'It implies they are not certain it was a suicide – they are not one hundred per cent sure.'

'Rubbish!' I said. 'They always say *"allegedly"*. They have to be careful, you know.'

But Sridhar wasn't even listening. He only said, 'Read this one, too,' and pushed the second clipping towards me.

'I can't read Tamil – yet.'

'I'll translate it for you then.'

He read it over once quickly and then began: 'A twenty-year-old girl, Sudha, hanged herself yesterday in the home of her relatives N. Sundararajan and his sister R. Janaki. Sudha, whose father was a priest at Thirukullam village, had been working for Sundararajan and Janaki for the past six months. The post-mortem reports indications of pregnancy but nothing conclusive has been said. Neighbours feel that she had been having an affair with Sundararajan.'

It sounded disgusting and sordid. I could hardly believe it was actually in the papers. It even occurred to me that Sridhar might be making all this up. Kodai was listening attentively to her brother though she'd probably read the reports already. When Sridhar finished she looked carefully at me as if it was important to her to see how I would react.

'Who told the newspaper people all this?' I asked.

'They just asked around, I suppose. A lot of people are talking about it.'

I took the clipping from him and looked at it carefully. The still unfamiliar alphabet danced before me, puzzling and tantalizingly cryptic. I wanted to be able to read it myself.

'What do they mean – they aren't sure if she was pregnant even after the post-mortem?'

'I don't know. Too early to say anything definite – or something like that.' Sridhar sounded uncertain. 'Anyway this is just a stupid little rag printed somewhere around here. This is precisely the kind of stuff they love.'

He suddenly looked guilty. 'You two go outside now,' he said abruptly, 'I have more important things to do. You can keep these if you want to.' I folded the clippings, put them into my pocket and ran down the steps. I could hear Kodai following me with heavy steps.

'I'll come back later,' I turned around to say. 'I have to go home – Janaki doesn't know I'm here.'

When I got home I looked under Sundar's bed, where he stored the old newspapers till they were sold at the end of every month. But someone had removed the *Hindu* of April 18th. I went to my room and pinned the clippings together and pushed them under my pile of books.

After that I made sure I read the newspaper carefully

every day for the next few weeks. People were concerned about the drought, a minister had resigned from the central government, the rupee's value had fallen further, gold chains had been snatched and wild elephants had gone on rampages. When I read the stories on Sudha's death it seemed the single most important and exciting thing in the world. Had everyone forgotten about it already or were they, too, waiting for something more to happen? It seemed strange that people could still want to know about all these other things. I knew that Sudha's death was the biggest thing that had ever happened on GC Street and that everyone here was still thinking and talking about it. And everything in the world seemed to be connected in some strange intricate way to Sudha and Sundar and Janaki. My father's project, the weather, my algebra formulae and the world that was whirling round us all at some wondrous speed.

'So you did come back,' Kodai said to me that evening, after Sridhar had shown me the newspaper clippings. 'I didn't think you would.'

'Didn't I say I would?' I said, feeling ashamed that I *had* come back.

'But that didn't mean you really meant to come,' Kodai persisted. 'You never liked to come here before, did you?' She looked at me suspiciously.

I was exasperated. 'All right, then, I'll go back home.'

'Wait!' Kodai called. 'I didn't say you should go home.'

Ambuja Pati, Kamala, Bhagya, Sulochana and Narayan Mama's daughter-in-law Vaishnavi were in Kamala's front room. Kamala looked very happy – this was what she liked best, to have people to talk to right there in her house, drinking the coffee she had made for them. And there was plenty to talk about that day. The fact that she lived right next door to Sundar and Janaki had given Kamala a special importance in the eyes of the neighbourhood.

'Are you sure you don't want anything to eat?' she was saying. 'It will only take me ten minutes, and . . .'

'No, no, sit down,' Sulochana said.

Kamala sat down but I could see that she couldn't understand why the others didn't want anything to eat with their coffee.

'I never thought such things could happen in Sundar's house,' Vaishnavi said.

Kodai later told me that Vaishnavi's parents had contemplated arranging her marriage with Sundar years ago, but Janaki's husband had died just then and nothing could be done right away. Vaishnavi, according to Kodai, had liked the idea and was still a little fascinated by and resentful of Sundar. That was why she was so loudly indignant and shocked now.

Kodai and I were still in the kitchen. I started to go in and join the women when she grabbed me by the shoulder.

'Let's wait here,' she hissed.

'But why?' I whispered back indignantly. I wanted to be able to hear them better.

'Just for a few minutes,' she insisted.

'That child, Sudha . . .' Bhagya was saying.

Ambuja Pati spoke up from her corner. She had been in her corner all along, her white brows drawn together in a contemptuous frown, as though she couldn't bear listening to the younger women's chatter.

'What do you mean, "child"? A whore – that's what she was.'

'Yes, yes,' Bhagya hastily apologized. 'And just think of it – a brahmin girl. That's what makes it so terrible.'

'Yes, my father-in-law was saying that if the women of the community begin to behave this way we are in trouble. It is we who uphold the deepest values of the culture,' Vaishnavi said importantly. The others nodded at that.

'And she was a priest's daughter, too,' Kamala said.

'I saw her the day before the day she died – with Nithya on the bus. I was with my brother,' Bhagya said. 'And you know what? I felt that she was avoiding me. She chose to sit as far away as possible though there were several seats right next to mine.'

'That's strange. Because she almost made it a *point* to talk to me,' Kamala began importantly. 'In fact it was just that morning that I was outside and . . . ' She had probably told them this story several times before, but everyone would have willingly listened to it all over again if Ambuja Pati hadn't cut her short.

'Enough of all this,' she said gruffly. 'What about Janaki? How is she taking it? Have any of you seen her?'

'Yes . . . poor Janaki,' the others sighed.

'I've asked you to tell her and come and see me, Kamala. Why doesn't she come here any more?' Ambuja Pati asked in a bewildered voice.

'She probably has a lot of work at home now, Amma,' Kamala said soothingly. 'I saw her a couple of times but she said she couldn't stop long.'

'She always liked to come and see me before . . .' Ambuja Pati said softly.

That's not true! I thought angrily. She *hated* it!

198

'But why did the girl kill herself?' Sulochana asked, steering them back to what mattered most.

'That's obvious, isn't it? She was pregnant. What else could she do?'

'And it was definitely Sundar?'

They were all very excited now.

'Who else could it have been? She never stepped out of that house on her own.'

'You can never say. Some of these servant girls are more sly than any of us know.'

'But Sudha was a *brahmin* girl,' Kamala said.

Everyone was quiet for a minute. The notes of a noisy film song reached them and then died down. A passing cyclist must have been carrying a transistor. Kodai stood behind me, damp, sweaty and fat. The faces of the women in the room were fair and very round. Rabbits, owlets, full moons.

'If it was Sundar . . .' Bhagya began.

'Of course it was,' Vaishnavi interrupted.

'Did Janaki know what was happening?' Bhagya continued.

'And that child – Padma's daughter.'

'Nithya? Nithya is very young. She wouldn't have understood anything,' Kamala said. She was sure she was right.

'But Janaki . . .' Sulochana shuddered. 'How terrible for her. But she couldn't have done much about it, I suppose. In her position – a widow, completely dependent on her brother.'

'The post-mortem wasn't properly done, and the police didn't ask enough questions,' said Sulochana. 'That's what my husband said. He says that Sundar must have given them something.'

'Why should he do that?'

Sulochana spoke cautiously. 'Maybe he had more to do with it than we think?'

'What do you mean?' Kamala asked.

She sounded genuinely puzzled. I strained forward to listen.

'I don't know. Maybe he could have . . .' Sulochana struggled.

'He could have what?' Vaishnavi asked excitedly.

'I don't know,' Sulochana admitted at last. 'I just wondered.'

I was an actress making a dramatic unannounced entrance. Kodai tried to stop me but I pulled myself away. The women saw me and stopped short.

'Coffee! You want coffee, Nithya?' Kamala struggled to get up. 'And is Kodai with you . . .?' Kodai ignored her mother's visitors and sat down in the chair on which Kamala had placed a pair of freshly ironed trousers.

'You're sitting on your father's clothes, Kodai,' Kamala protested, and tried to pull them from below her. Kodai didn't move an inch.

'Get up from that chair, Kodai!' her grandmother said sharply. Kodai got up and went upstairs but came down again very soon. She later told me that Ambuja Pati had been especially angry with her that morning because she had caught Kodai making secret sketches in a notebook the day before and demanded that Kodai show them to her. Kodai had refused and had ripped out the sheet of paper, crumpled it up and thrown it away. She wouldn't even tell me what the pictures were, and I didn't care to ask.

'No, I don't want coffee,' I said when Kamala thrust

some at me. Kamala looked like she didn't know what to do with it and then drank it herself, raising the tumbler high above her mouth to make sure the rim didn't touch her lips.

They sat around uneasily, not sure how to continue the conversation. I knew that they wanted to ask me a hundred questions but didn't know if they should.

'So how are things at home, Nithya?' Bhagya asked.

I stared, not saying anything. She looked abashed.

'How are Sundar and Janaki?' Sulochana asked.

'They're fine.'

The atmosphere in the room had suddenly deflated, as if all that excitement and curiosity had gone out of the window with a weak, almost inaudible hiss. That's not what I had intended.

'Though I sometimes think Janaki is not feeling well,' I ventured.

Their eyes brightened and they clicked their tongues sympathetically.

'Poor thing! What's the matter with her?' Kamala said. 'And she has all the housework on her hands now.'

'Or is it because of Sundar and Sudha?' Vaishnavi asked. The others frowned in disapproval. It wasn't right to ask a child such a question. But they still waited for me to answer.

'No, it's not that,' I said. 'It's other things.'

'What are you trying to say?' Ambuja Pati asked sternly. 'What other things?'

'I don't know.' I was startled to hear my voice trembling.

The ceiling fan stopped – the electricity had failed – but no one exclaimed or seemed even to notice. Only

Kamala began fanning herself vigorously with a rolled-up magazine. I saw that Ambuja Pati was watching me with half-shut eyes, which made her look older and more cunning than ever. It occurred to me that she barely had eyelashes.

'I don't know,' I said again, very slowly and deliberately. 'But I'm frightened.'

'Of what?' Sulochana asked. *Her* voice was now trembling.

'Of Sundar,' I heard myself say, remarkably steadily.

'But why?' they asked, almost in chorus.

*   *   *

And in the middle of all that was happening, one afternoon after Janaki had made me my three o'clock cup of coffee and gone upstairs, I pushed open the back door and a white cow thrust its enormous face into mine. I stepped back, startled, and shut the door quickly. I heard the cow puff and sigh outside and the door rattle – it was trying to get in. I wondered if I should go upstairs and tell Janaki but decided to go investigate for myself.

I slipped out through the front of the house and ran back into the garden. It was still at the kitchen door and it wasn't a cow at all, I realized after looking carefully – it was a bull. His long, curved horns were like tusks and were covered with red paint that was beginning to peel. He turned from the door and looked at me. I backed away and stood behind a tree. He was the tallest bull I'd ever seen, over five feet from the ground, I guessed, with a huge hump and great flaps of skin hanging from below his neck. His skin was clean and milk-white, not dung-splattered like other animals'. He began eating the short, dry grass and the withered white flowers with yellow middles which grew in the garden sometimes. He looked peaceful and happy out in the sunlight by himself, almost unreal, like the bull whose back the girl in the Greek story had got onto and flown over the sea on, away from her father and two brothers.

I crouched behind the tree and watched him, but he continued to eat quietly and there was nothing for me to do. I didn't dare move closer to him, though I knew Sudha wouldn't have hesitated. So I went back inside.

Janaki came downstairs later. I remembered the bull and followed her into the kitchen. She went out to fill the water pot and I waited for her to see him.

'There's a bull in our garden!' she said when she came back. I'd never heard her sound so surprised. But she didn't shut the door, so we both stood and watched. The bull seemed to be thirsty – he pushed his face into one of the two iron buckets kept near the pump and it fell to the ground with a rattle.

'He was there even earlier this afternoon,' I told Janaki.

'And you didn't tell anyone?' she asked, looking at me curiously.

'He wasn't doing any harm.'

'Didn't Raju see him?'

'Raju came in early today. He handed over the milk at two o'clock.'

'We have to get it out of here,' she said.

'Shall I get someone from Kodai's house to help?'

Janaki hesitated. 'Let's see if we can get him out ourselves.'

But when we went out, Kamala was already there with Vasu and Narayan Mama, who had probably stopped by.

'Oh, Janaki, there you are! I saw the bull and called the men out. We were wondering if you had seen it,' Kamala said.

'Do you know who it belongs to?' Janaki asked.

'No one on *our* street owns a bull,' Narayan Mama said. 'It has broken loose from one of the carts near the marketplace or has come from one of the fields outside town.'

The bull reached up and pulled at the leaves of the mango tree.

'You should get him out before he eats up your garden,' Vasu said. He hitched his veshti up his thin legs and climbed over the bushes.

I wished they would leave the bull alone. He had come suddenly and mysteriously out of some place we didn't know, and I wanted him to stay longer. Vasu looked like he didn't know what to do now that he had got into Janaki's garden.

'Be careful,' Kamala shouted out. 'He looks really strong.'

'Yes, please be careful,' Janaki said.

Vasu picked up a stick from the ground.

'Ay!' he shouted. 'Get out of here!'

The bull looked at him in surprise. Vasu struck at his behind, timidly at first and then sharply. The bull turned its head and I thought it was going to lunge at Vasu but it turned away and, lowering its great white head, rushed across the yard with a bellow. It looked like it was heading towards Kamala's house. She yelped in terror, and both she and Narayan Mama leapt out of the way and rushed in. But the bull changed direction and crashed through the row of bushes that separated our house from the street behind. With its tail held stiff and high, it galloped down the road for a couple of yards and then slowed to a walk, its bony haunches pale orange in the sunset.

'What is happening here?' Sundar had come back home and was standing near the kitchen door. It looked like no one was going to answer him. Then Janaki said, 'Nothing. A bull got into our garden and Vasu chased him away.'

Kamala was staring at Sundar with undisguised curiosity. Even Narayan Mama was looking at him from under his grey beetle brows, his eyes stern and narrow beneath the spectacles I liked to think he wore only for effect. Kamala opened her mouth, but Vasu told her something under his breath and they turned around and went into their house. Narayan Mama followed them and shut the door firmly. None of them had said a word to Sundar.

Sundar shut the door behind the three of us. He looked very slightly hurt, but he smiled at me and said in a loud, cheerful voice quite unlike his, 'Well, you got rid of the bull, anyway!'

But when I looked out of an upstairs window later that day I saw that the bull had trampled down some of the bushes. The house and garden looked naked and exposed to the world, as though the walls had collapsed.

*　　　*　　　*

So there was suddenly more to talk about regarding Sudha's death and whatever else could have happened in Sundar's house. But it wasn't as if I had told them all that much, really.

'Why are you frightened of Sundar?' Kamala and the others had asked me that evening, and I hadn't known what to say.

'I don't know,' was all I had said again and again, till they were puzzled and irritated and didn't try to stop me when I got up and said that I was going home.

*   *   *

When I saw Sulochana and Vaishnavi go into Kodai's house one evening a few days after that, I ran out into Kodai's garden. The kitchen door was open.

'Kodai!' I called into the house.

'Is that you, Nithya?' Kamala called back.

I could see right through the kitchen into the front room, where Kamala was sitting with her two visitors.

'Kodai is not at home, but why don't you come in?' she invited.

'I'll come back later,' I said.

But I didn't go home. I sat outside in the fast-descending darkness and listened to the three women talking. They had loud voices and these rooms were smaller than the ones in Janaki's house.

'It's strange that Nithya said she was frightened of Sundar. I was telling my husband about it and he thinks so, too.'

'Of course it is strange.'

'He should have been married long ago – that's why all this trouble started. I always wondered why he wasn't married.'

'Even my father-in-law mama who dislikes talking about things of this kind says it really looks like

206

Sundar had more to do with the death than we know. What other reason could Nithya have to be frightened of him?'

They had lowered their voices now. I slipped into the kitchen. Kamala might decide to come in to fetch something but I would worry about that when it happened.

'Do you think Sudha was killed?' Kamala asked in a frightened voice.

It was a warm evening but I felt my spine prickle. I had only vaguely anticipated this. The conclusions they had arrived at horrified and thrilled me. And it wasn't entirely my doing – they wanted it to have happened this way. Willed themselves into believing it.

'Maybe he didn't actually kill her. The police would have been able to make that out – I think,' Vaishnavi said. 'But he might have got her to kill herself – or something like that. He might have said that it was the best thing to do under the circumstances, and she might have been so frightened that she did it.'

'But why should he want to do that?'

'He was frightened.'

They were all quiet, as if they too were frightened now.

'Maybe he *helped* her kill herself. He came home early from work on the day she died – remember?'

Of course they remembered.

A gate, either Kamala's or Janaki's, creaked open. It was nearly six in the evening, time for both Sundar and Vasu to return. I was out of the room and back home in a minute. No one had seen me, but I had been bitten by mosquitoes and I scratched at the red marks they left behind for the rest of the evening.

'Helping someone commit suicide is a crime,' Kodai came to tell me two days later. 'Narayan Mama has found that out. A person who does that can be arrested by the police.'

It was through Kodai that I learnt much of what people were talking about. Everyone was sorry for Janaki because she was trapped inside that house with her brother, they were anxious about me sometimes and those who passed by the house looked up at the upstairs windows and wondered . . . Even Kamala didn't like coming out into her garden after dark, as she had started imagining strange, shadowy shapes among her neighbour's trees and bushes.

*　　*　　*

Kodai took me down the street with her one evening. 'I saw someone when I came up this way a few minutes ago – he might still be there,' she said.

Kodai would often go on short expeditions down the road and the nearby streets without letting her mother know. Kamala assumed she was at one of the neighbours' houses, and Ambuja Pati had stopped caring.

Janaki came in just when the two of us were setting out.

'Where are you both going?' she asked.

'To Kodai's house,' I lied.

I guessed that the person Kodai had seen was Raghu. He was still standing at the end of the road. I remembered that the last time I had seen him, it had been raining and Sudha had been alive. When he saw Kodai and me, he walked up to us swinging his short muscled arms.

'She is Janaki's niece,' Kodai said importantly, point-
ing to me.

'I know,' he said.

He wasn't smiling his nervous little smile that day. I
thought he looked troubled.

'I was very sorry to hear about that poor child,' he
told me softly.

I stared at him. People were saying many things
about Sudha but I hadn't heard anyone talk of her
that way, with so much kindness and understanding,
except perhaps Sridhar that time I went up to his
room. I was startled to feel tears prickle somewhere
behind my eyes, though I didn't cry.

If Raghu hadn't been so aware that he was deformed
and half-caste, and if this hadn't been Thiruninravur,
he might have reached for my hands and held them in
sympathy between his own two little tough palms.

Chapter Ten

He wanted to know if there was any way he could see Janaki.

'Ask her if I can visit,' he urged. 'She'll remember me – we were in college together.'

He sounded distraught. The rumours and gossip must have reached him, and he, like the others, must believe that Janaki was frightened.

'Tell her I'll be able to help her,' he said. I wasn't sure what he meant.

'Do this for her sake – and for mine,' he told me urgently when I didn't reply.

'I'll see,' I said uncertainly. I wondered why I wasn't refusing him right away, and how I would get Janaki to agree to see him.

He seemed reassured by what I said. 'I knew you would help. I'll be around here most evenings. Send Kodai if you can't come yourself.' And for the first time that evening he smiled.

Kodai hadn't spoken. 'Are you really going to ask Janaki to let him meet her?' she asked me after Raghu left.

'I don't know. I don't think so.'

I didn't want Kodai to have anything more to do with this and was grateful when she didn't ask any more questions.

* * *

Janaki noticed that I was coming in through the front door. Anyone who went to the neighbours' house usually came back through the kitchen.

But she only said, 'I was beginning to wonder if you were going to eat at Kamala's place tonight.'

I learnt that they had locked Sudha's room while I was ill. Janaki and I unlocked it the next day. The police had told us to wait two weeks after the death before we disturbed the room, and we had already waited much longer. It was Janaki who took the key from her cupboard and turned around to me. I was standing behind her, watching.

'Do you want to come with me?' she asked.

'Yes.'

The room was exactly as it had been the last time I had seen it except that a layer of red-brown dust had settled on the bed and the floor, blurring the circle of chalk. The windows were still shut tight. It bothered me. Sudha had never liked her windows shut.

'Shall I open the windows?' I asked Janaki.

'Yes, let's let some fresh air in.' Janaki kept her own windows open now and let the sari-curtains flutter whenever there was a breeze. She began to strip Sudha's bed of its sheets and pillowcase.

'Are you going to wash them?'

'They need to be burnt,' Janaki said very softly, and I remembered how she hadn't raised her voice even when she had spoken to Sudha that last time. She was now carefully sweeping the floor. I wondered if it would have made any difference if I had chosen to tell the neighbours other things.

'Won't there be a court hearing? Won't they need to see all this?' I asked.

'There won't be a hearing. And anyway the police have records of everything they saw here.'

She went downstairs carrying the sheets with her. She placed them in a small crumpled pile in the garden, sprinkled kerosene on them and lit a match. She stood close to the fire. The heat didn't seem to bother her and the smoke bellowed around her in a black silken tent. Kamala saw it and came out. She wanted to talk to us but someone called out to her and she went in. When she had finished whatever she had been called in to do, she didn't come right outside but stationed herself by her open kitchen window and watched.

The sheets burnt very quickly. Janaki gathered what was left behind in a basket that Raju would empty the next day. I looked back to see if we had left any sparks behind us – if we had, the fire would spread rapidly from one dry leaf to another, would roll across the garden and push its way into the house, making the walls shudder and fall to the ground in a storm of hissing and crackling, and would leave a heap of burnt plaster and soot-covered stone. I wondered if Janaki would be upset if the house she had been born in, grown up in, left and then returned to was destroyed.

'I saw your friend Raghu,' I told her just before we went back inside. I wanted to see if that would

212

surprise her. Maybe Janaki already knew that Raghu had been fond of her in college.

But she only asked, 'Raghu? The . . . ?'

Dwarf. I knew that that's what she had been thinking. I nodded.

She didn't go straight up as I thought she would. She sat down on the kitchen floor and leaned against the wall. The sun shone in through the open door. She was waiting for me to say something more.

'He wanted to see you. He wanted to know if you would agree to see him.'

'He told you that?'

'Yes, he wanted to see you – badly.'

Janaki got up and poured herself some water.

'Did he tell you why?' She drank one glass of water and then another. She must have been very thirsty.

'No, he didn't, but . . .'

I wanted her to ask me to go on, but she didn't.

'He felt he should come,' I said at last.

*   *   *

When I walked down the road that evening, Raghu was not there as he had promised. I was annoyed – what did he mean by saying he would come and then not coming? It would serve him right if I never told him that Janaki had not objected to his coming to see her. Just when I was about to go back home he ran up, panting. He'd probably rushed from the bus stand. He looked up at me expectantly and I stared back at him without speaking. That seemed to make him nervous.

'She said you could come,' I said.

He looked surprised, as if he hadn't really expected that. 'When? Right away?'

213

Janaki hadn't said anything about when. 'Tomorrow morning. She wants you to come tomorrow morning after eleven o'clock.' I knew Sundar would be away at work then.

Raghu didn't stay much longer after that. I lingered outside for a while, contemplated going to see Kodai, wondered why I hadn't seen Sridhar for so many days now and then went back home.

When Raghu knocked at the back door the next morning it was Janaki who opened it. She seemed taken aback and stood looking down at him without speaking.

'Come in,' she said at last, and led the way into the front room. He looked around for a chair, and when he didn't find one he sat against the wall, his short legs stretched out before him. Janaki sat on the other side of the room and I stood in a corner from which I could look at both of them.

Raghu seemed tongue-tied. Janaki, too, did not speak. After looking at me once or twice as if he hoped I would say something, he began telling Janaki how upset he was about everything that had happened. I wondered what he was talking about – Sudha's death? Or the things that had happened to Janaki since they had last spoken to each other all those years ago?

Because I remembered the shrill, raucous voice of the midget I had once heard at a circus, I had forgotten that Raghu had a different kind of voice, measured and surprisingly deep. He probably didn't have anyone to talk with at home. Perhaps that's why Janaki meant so much more to him now – she too was alone.

When I looked at her she was frowning and looking at Raghu very carefully. What did she think of him, her first very own guest in seven years? But it was never easy to say what Janaki was thinking.

When she stayed silent, Raghu seemed worried that he had upset or offended her. 'It is very hot this year,' he said helplessly.

'Yes, it is very hot.' She hesitated before asking, 'Would you like to drink some water?'

'No, no,' he said hurriedly, though he was sweating heavily. 'I don't need anything. I've just eaten.'

'But you can have some water,' Janaki said, and went into the kitchen. I stayed where I was and saw Raghu look quickly around the room and at the pictures on the wall, as if he hoped that they would tell him something more about this woman he had watched and thought about for so many years. Janaki returned with a tall glass of water on a plate, which she placed on the floor at his side. Later that afternoon, after Raghu had left, I came down to the kitchen to see if I could find out whether Janaki had given Raghu one of the glasses we drank from or one of those she kept aside. But that was yet another thing I never discovered.

He didn't drink the water anyway. He had made up his mind to talk.

'Do you remember that year in college – the first year BA?' he smiled shyly.

'Yes,' Janaki said, and he looked grateful.

'I don't live here,' he then confessed. 'My house is about seven miles from this street.' As if he felt it was important to remind her that he couldn't be counted as one of us. Janaki only nodded.

'Well, maybe I should be going now,' he said after about ten minutes during which they had talked a little about college and what my parents were doing in Kuwait. He looked as if he hoped Janaki would ask him to stay longer. When she didn't he said, 'I am very thankful to Nithya for telling you everything.' He looked at me and smiled.

'Everything?' Janaki asked softly.

He looked confused at that, but when he spoke again he simply said, 'About how important it was for me to see you again.'

It was only because I was looking at Janaki so carefully that I noticed a spark of something fly up to her eyes for a very brief second. But I wasn't sure what it was – delight or shock or anger or revulsion.

'You should let me know if you need help, any kind of help,' Raghu said, and he got up to go.

Janaki led the way through the kitchen and I followed. When Raghu looked up at her before opening the door she actually smiled at him faintly.

'I'll contact you,' she said, 'and you should come here again sometime.'

From the garden, where I had slipped while they were talking to each other, I saw his face brighten. He smiled, and looked like a nice little boy with a big head and a strange body who had had to wear spectacles too soon.

No one had seen him enter or leave the house. Janaki and I didn't tell anyone about the visit, either, though Kodai asked me again if I had told Janaki what Raghu had said.

'No, I haven't. I don't want to,' I said contemptuously.

'But he waits at the end of the road. I see him every day,' she said.

216

'Let him wait. No one is asking him to come,' I said. A couple of days after he came to our house I went to see if she was right, and there he was. But I didn't yet have a message from Janaki.

I knew she had not forgotten him, that he was there in some part of the quiet furious spiral of thoughts in her head. I would sometimes come into the kitchen and see her sitting at the stove as if she had forgotten there was something on it. The steam would be hot and wet on her face, covering her forehead and upper lip with tiny beads of sweat. Something – something new – drove her restlessness into an energy that made her get up every morning and go back to bed so exhausted that she slept right through the night.

She sometimes went out during the day, though she'd never been out by herself before. I followed her once to see where she was going, but she took a bus and I couldn't risk being discovered by getting on myself.

One day when Janaki was not at home, Sundar came in at midday. He too had changed now – he looked tired even before he left for work and his clothes were limp on him, either because Janaki had stopped ironing them or because he was getting thinner.

'Why have you come home early, Sundar Mama?' I asked him.

'I wasn't feeling well,' he said without looking at me, and began climbing the stairs.

I waited for a minute before telling him, 'Janaki is not at home.'

He stopped, turned around and looked down at me. 'Where is she?'

'I don't know,' I said.

'Has she gone out by herself?'

'Yes.' I enjoyed the bewilderment on his face.

When Janaki returned I told her that Sundar had come home early.

'He asked for you,' I said. 'I told him you had gone out.'

This didn't seem to worry her. Maybe she had actually been waiting for this to happen.

Sundar must have heard the door opening because he came down at once. 'Where have you been?' He looked at Janaki carefully. Maybe he too noticed that she had begun to tie her hair more loosely around her face than before.

'I went out to check my bank account.'

Sundar's eyes narrowed. 'Why did you have to do that? Don't I look after your money?'

'I needed to see for myself.' She looked steadily at him. 'There was much less money than I thought there would be. They said you had drawn five thousand rupees over the last few months alone. I didn't know it was that much when you asked me to sign those cheques.'

'There have been expenses. I don't earn enough to cover them all.'

'But I wish I had been told how much you were taking out. You have forgotten – it is my money. Amma gave it to me after selling my jewellery.'

'And you too have forgotten many things.' He spoke as calmly as she had. 'That I am in charge of your affairs since the day your husband died and you chose to come back here because you told Amma that it was becoming impossible for you to live any longer there with your in-laws. You have suddenly forgotten what is proper to your position. You know you cannot go out by yourself. Look at Vasu's mother – people look on her with a respect they won't have for you much longer if you go on this way.'

He stopped as if he expected her to say something. When she didn't he went on: 'I have noticed that you don't go to see Ambuja Pati any more, either.'

'You can tell her that that I may not visit her again. She has nothing to tell me that I want to listen to.'

She too hadn't raised her voice but the brilliance of her anger slammed against his face like something big and hard. He looked as if he wanted to say something else but stopped abruptly. He turned and saw me.

'What are you doing here?' It was the only time he had ever spoken roughly to me. 'I don't want you listening to this. Go up to your room.'

I didn't move but looked at Janaki, who didn't even look at me but said, 'Let her stay. I don't see why she should go. I want her here.'

Sundar went to the door as if he had finished saying what he wanted to.

'I saw that you received an invitation for Raman's daughter's wedding. Are you going?' I wondered why she asked him that now.

'The wedding is in Madras,' he replied.

'Yes, but are you going?'

'I'm not.'

'What are you afraid of? That people will talk about you – the man who slept with a little servant girl?' Janaki said softly.

I saw him flinch. Without looking at Janaki he said stiffly, 'There is plenty people could say about you if I decided to let them know. But I see it as my duty to look after you. I've seen it that way ever since you returned home.'

He went out of the room and Janaki's laughter rippled in one smooth soft wave through the house. It was the first time I had heard her laugh aloud.

*   *   *

She went up after a while and lay down. I sat with a book on my lap and thought about the quarrel. I waited for Janaki to say something to me but she didn't. Why had she said that she wanted me in the room? What difference did my being there make to her? I couldn't work out whom I preferred – the grim, quiet, lonely woman I had seen when I first came here or this new Janaki. Something frightening and fascinating had happened. When I was much younger that was how I had felt about some of the things that could possibly happen to my world – like Amma cutting her hair very short.

But right now it was important to stay still and wait. I looked across at Janaki. She had her eyes closed, though I didn't think she was asleep.

After a while I went out. Sundar's room was shut and when I put my ear against the door there was no sound inside. There was nothing to see in the third room. After Janaki had cleaned it some days ago I had looked inside just once – it had been stripped of everything but the bare mattress. I imagined how if anyone stood in the middle of it and shut the door and shouted, the sounds would bounce jerkily off the walls and slam back.

I went downstairs and opened the front door. There was no one outside on the street and I was about to go back in when I saw Sridhar walking with his head low, carrying an umbrella.

'Sridhar!' I called softly. He stopped and looked at me. 'Where are you going?' I asked. He seemed ill that day. His face was red and perspiring in spite of the umbrella.

'Nowhere,' he muttered, and he walked on faster than before.

I was vaguely indignant that he hadn't stopped to talk to me, but I was too preoccupied that afternoon to care much. I went back into the house, shut the door and stood there wondering what to do next. A faint breeze rippled in through the open kitchen window. It toppled a small vessel someone had left on the floor and sighed through the front room. I went back to the garden to see if it had really got cooler.

It had. The sun had gone behind a cloud and the light in the garden was grey and a soft undersea green. It was very quiet. Even the birds seemed surprised by the sudden change – they had stopped twittering. But even as I walked under the trees the sun came out again, hotter and brighter than before. A crow cawed. A dozen other crows cawed back hysterically from some other garden, and this one flew towards the sound. I knew that something was wrong because that's why crows caw together this way, in raspy chorus. One of them was dead or hurt.

But they stopped abruptly and I wandered through the trees to see Lakshmi. I made sure to visit her at least once a day now. She was flicking her tail half-heartedly – she never seemed to do anything, day after day after day. It was hard to know if she was bored, if she ever wanted to break through the flimsy walls of her shed and race through the garden like that bull had done with lowered head and glinting horns. Lakshmi too had horns, long, sharp brown ones that curved out from the sides of her head. They used to make me nervous. But she seemed happy enough to stand there looking out at the sun and the trees, oblivious to the huge pile of dung that gathered behind her and would not be carted away till the evening.

A huge white flower seemed to have sprung out of the ground where the snake gourd plant had been. When I got closer I saw that it had sprung out of the single tough cord of a new creeper. It didn't look like a snake gourd this time. I knelt down to look at it. I had seen this plant once before – it was a pumpkin. Sudha had planted a pumpkin creeper without telling any of us about it. Sundar liked pumpkin, she had said, and Janaki had said they could think about it later. I ran my finger around the inside of the flower. It was the biggest flower I had ever seen, and when I bent to smell it was like dipping my face into a bowl. It had a strange, fresh, bitter smell. When I looked up from it the sun shone straight into my face, making my eyes water.

Through the film of tears I thought I saw the blurred figure of someone walking at the other end of the garden and heard the crunch of dry coconut flowers below their feet. It was a young woman. She carried a basket at her waist and wore a cotton sari, and I knew that her hair wouldn't grow much below her waist. She disappeared behind one of the coconut trees, and when I went closer I saw that she was sweeping the leaves and dry flowers into her basket. But just as I was about to call out her name she got up, pushing a strand of hair behind her ears just as she used to a long, long time ago. She then walked away, into the house or down the lane, behind or into the tamarind trees, or simply to wander through the hot, bright streets of Thiruninravur.

I looked around. Nothing seemed different in the garden and the sparrows continued their chirping. I wondered if the ground beneath the coconut trees was disturbed. I sat under one of them and allowed the tears to fall down my cheeks and drip softly, saltily into the corners of my mouth. It was the first time I let myself mourn Sudha. And it was a moment of being alone, away from everything else.

*　　*　　*

Someone knocked at the front door the next day, about an hour after Sundar had left the house. Neither Janaki nor Sundar had said anything more to each other the day before. When it was time for him to eat, she had placed his plate and the vessels of food on the ground and gone upstairs. He had come down, looked around the kitchen, served himself and begun to eat while I watched him from the front room. He must have found something cold because he got up and placed it on the stove as if he meant to reheat it, but then changed his mind and ate it just as it was.

I heard the knock and opened the door before Janaki could come down. It was a police constable, a different one from the two who had come the day of the death.

'Is Sundararajan at home?' he asked.

I shook my head, and he looked like he didn't know what to do. His shirt was frayed at the sleeves and his calves were fat and very hairy beneath his shorts.

223

'Is anyone else at home, then? Doesn't his sister also live here?'

'Yes, I am here.' I hadn't heard Janaki come down.

I caught a glimpse of Kamala on the other side of the compound wall. I knew she could hear everything that was being said.

'Why don't you come in?' Janaki said. He stepped reluctantly into the house and stood just inside the door, fanning himself with a damp handkerchief.

'What's the matter?' she asked.

'We need to speak to your brother. I was asked to take him with me to the station for questioning.'

'Regarding the girl's death?'

'Yes, the girl's death.'

'But I thought all that was settled at that time. The girl killed herself. Your sub-inspector said it has been registered as a case of suicide.'

'Yes, but it was our sub-inspector who sent me here. He said we need to ask Sundar a few questions.' He spoke gently to her though she was neither nervous or excited.

'Do you know why this has happened – all of a sudden?' she asked.

'There are rumours that your brother had something more to do with the death than we suspected.'

'Do they think he killed her?'

I hadn't expected her to ask him that and even he seemed surprised by it, and at how calm she was. But I sensed that she was starting to be frightened.

'No, no,' he said, sounding embarrassesd. 'And anyway, I don't know if I should tell you all this. I was only given instructions to bring Sundararajan to the station for questioning. There has been some pressure on the sub-inspector.'

'From whom?'

'From people – people around here,' he said vaguely. 'Our sub-inspector has been accused of letting the case rest too quickly, of taking too many things for granted.'

He might have told us even more if Janaki hadn't cut him short. 'My brother will be home only this evening. He is away at work.'

'I'll come back for him later, then,' the constable said, and he turned to go. He already had his hand on the latch when he asked, 'Have you disturbed the room upstairs?'

'We were told that we could clear up ten days after she died. We waited much longer than that.'

'I was told to take a look at it again.'

I knew Janaki was beginning to unnerve him. We followed him upstairs and stood at Sudha's door to watch him. I already knew there was nothing for him to see. He looked quickly at the bare walls and clean floor and nodded a little helplessly.

'Someone will come to look at it again later – maybe. I'll go now and return in the evening,' he said.

Just as he was pushing open the gate, I ran up to him. He looked at me enquiringly. 'Are you going to arrest Sundar Mama?' I asked.

'No, no,' he said reassuringly. 'No arrest. We just want him to come to the station for questioning.'

He had parked his bicycle just outside the gate. I watched him wobble down the street.

Janaki had been at the door all the while and had heard my question and the constable's reply. She looked like she was about to tell me something but changed her mind and went out to the bathroom. She was in there for a long time and when she got back her hair was wet.

I was almost sure the police would decide to go straight to Sundar's office to get him. But a constable turned up again in the evening, a different one – tall and mean, with a little wisp of a moustache.

'Sundar has just got back from office. He is washing himself,' I said. It was true. Neither Janaki nor I had had time to tell him anything.

'Tell him I'm here.' He was rude, I thought. 'And tell him I can't wait long.'

Sundar came in just then, wiping his hands. 'Is something the matter?' he asked.

'Does this child have to be here, listening to every-thing?' the policeman asked, looking at me in irritation.

'Go in, Nithya.'

But I didn't go in, I stood a little farther inside the room and listened to the policeman speak to Sundar. I knew Janaki was listening from the kitchen.

Sundar didn't even seem surprised. 'Why don't you go ahead?' he said. 'I'll come in a few minutes.'

'I was given orders to make sure you came back with me,' the constable said. 'Our sub-inspector is tired of people talking – accusing him of all kinds of things.'

Sundar nodded and went upstairs. When he came down he had changed back into his shirt and trousers.

'Shall we take the scooter?'

'No, we can walk.'

And they went down the street together, the tall, straight-shouldered policeman and Sundar, who kept his eyes fixed on the ground and walked with a stoop I hadn't noticed before.

And they had all come out to their doorsteps to watch: Narayan Mama, Vasu, Kamala, Seshadri, Sulochana, Gopal, Bhagya, Vaishnavi and half a dozen others. Those who were not at home then, who were still away at work or at the market or out of town, would be told all about it as soon as they returned. No one said anything or asked any questions right then; they only looked, standing at their gates and front doors.

*　　*　　*

'Dead Girl's Employer Questioned by Police.' That was the headline of the last news report Kodai gave me, along with Sridhar's written translation.

'Thiruninravur. May 5th. N. Sundararajan, who was the employer and distant relative of twenty-year-old Sudha, who killed herself on April 18th on Govindachari Street, was taken to Thiruninravur Police Station for questioning. Neighbours of the family suspected foul play and according to them, Sundararajan, who was having a affair with Sudha, aided and abetted the suicide or Sudha killed herself under pressure from him. Sudha might have been pregnant when she died. Police sub-inspector K. L. Hariharan, who was handling the case, said that Sundararajan was sent back home in a short while. "There is no conclusive evidence that points to anything other than suicide, nor is there any proof that the dead girl was pressurized into killing herself. We cannot make any arrests and have decided to close the case," he said. However some of the residents on GC

Street are still not satisfied. Sundar himself refused to speak to our reporter.'

'My brother didn't want to do this.' Kodai pointed to the translation. 'He is very busy nowadays. I begged him to – for your sake.'

I didn't thank her or even say anything. It had been nearly eight o'clock when Sundar had got back home that evening. The neighbours had lingered outside for quite a while, waiting for him to return or for another policeman to come with the news that he had been arrested. But it had grown dark and they had had to go inside and wait for whatever news the next day would bring.

That was why Sundar was able to come back un-observed. He looked exhausted, even ill. He went straight upstairs without eating and didn't come down till the next afternoon. For the next three days he didn't go to work or even leave the house. And all the while he didn't say a word to either of us.

Kodai later told me that her father said there'd been some idea that the police talk to Janaki and me as well. But Sundar had begged them not to; he might have even bribed them heavily. Almost no one else wanted to pursue the matter, and those who did were persuaded not to. It was not a nice thing for a widow or a young girl, they'd said. And anyway, nothing was likely to come of it.

Chapter Eleven

I helped Janaki clean up. Utensils that hadn't been used for years, giant cumbersome copper ones, were dragged outdoors to be washed and polished. When we finished, the sunlight glinted off their surfaces and shot into my eyes.

'What are we going to do with these now?' I asked. 'Will you put them back inside?'

'We'll find someone who'll use them, or we'll sell them. We don't really need them any more.'

We dusted the house, even the top of the ceiling fan and the backs of the pictures. We were priests performing a ceremony, an elaborate cleansing ritual. Upstairs, we cleared Janaki's cupboard and pushed the sacks of rice and tamarind in the storeroom into neat orderly lines, upsetting dozens of centipedes. cockroaches and what looked to me like minia-ture scorpions, which ran around in panic till Janaki gathered them up and threw them into the far end of the garden.

When we finished she threw away our dust-wreathed

brooms and rags and we drew buckets of water from the well and splashed it over the stone and cement floors, making them cool and clean. Only Sundar's room was left untouched.

But Sundar himself had changed. He stayed in his room all the time he was at home coming down only for his lonely meals. He'd even stopped going to look over his land as often as he used to. One or two grey strands appeared at his temples, and when he was kneeling down to buckle his sandals one day I noticed that the hair on the back of his head was thinning. The neighbours would have little to do with him, I noticed. One morning I saw Narayan Mama bump into him, lower his head determinedly and walk on. Even the children stared and whispered when he passed them.

'Janaki and I are busy cleaning up and I hardly ever go out nowadays . . .' I wrote in the last letter I sent my parents that summer.

It was true – I didn't go out any more to see Kodai or Sridhar or even to stand at the gate. I hadn't yet finished the books I'd brought with me but school and home seemed far away, a hazy cloud that receded further every day.

But Kodai seemed to want someone to talk to. She knocked on our door one morning and I opened it.

'There is plenty happening at home,' Kodai said. She peered over my shoulder into the house, probably hoping to catch a glimpse of Sundar. Before I could decide whether I wanted to let her in, she had stepped into the kitchen. I reluctantly led the way to the front room.

'What's happening?' I asked her. I might as well

know if I was going to be stuck with her for the evening.

'Sridhar is acting strange. He doesn't even want to talk to me any more,' Kodai said sadly. 'He's had two big quarrels with Appa, Amma and Pati.'

'About what?'

'He has finished his final exams. He is sure to do well. He'll probably even get a rank.' I knew that was meant to impress me.

'Maybe he will. But you haven't told me what the quarrels were about,' I said.

'He wants to go away, to Madras. To look for a job or to study. They want him to stay on here. And Appa says anyway there are no scholarships left for brahmin boys.' She was panting with the effort of talking so much. 'I want Sridhar to stay at home, too.' And her face suddenly crumpled.

'Why should it matter to you?' I asked her, feeling both irritated and embarrassed. 'He's only your brother.' She sniffed.

She looked up in surprise when a loud voice chattered excitedly through a buzz of static, announcing a Tamil film song. It was Janaki's new transistor.

'Is that *Janaki* listening to the radio?' Kodai asked.

'Yes,' I said. Her eyes widened. She seemed to have forgotten that she had been crying.

'And what else is happening in your house?' I asked. If Kodai had nothing more to say she should go home.

'My pati is very ill,' she said nonchalantly. 'She's been ill for quite a while now but it's been worse since yesterday.'

*   *   *

231

Ambuja Pati couldn't ever be ill. In spite of her frail little body, she was as tough as a rock and about as ancient. She would go on for ever.

'She has a stomach problem,' Kodai continued. 'The doctor came in yesterday. He said it was a bad case of *diarrhoea*.' Kodai pronounced the word carefully. 'And Appa says it is all Sridhar's fault.'

And it looked like Ambuja Pati got still worse that day. She was admitted to hospital early that evening. A rickety old hired car drew up at Vasu's door and Ambuja Pati was carried into it. Vasu sat next to the driver and the car creaked and heaved as Kamala got into the back to be with her mother-in-law.

'Do you know what has happened?' Janaki asked. She hadn't come out but was looking through a window.

'Kodai's grandmother is not well. They are taking her to hospital.'

There was no further news of her till the next morning. We were out in the garden when Kamala came, all excited and out of breath.

'Oh, Janaki, I have been waiting to see you! I wanted to tell you that my mother-in-law is very ill and in hospital.'

'Yes, I know. Nithya told me, and we saw the ambulance yesterday,' Janaki said.

'She seems better now – though it has cost us two hundred rupees for medicine alone so far . . .'

'I thought you had gone to be with her?'

'My husband and I take it in turns to go. Sridhar is always out and Kodai is alone at home. We don't like to leave a growing girl alone, you know.'

She turned to smile at me. 'Nithya, too, is growing up.'

232

'Maybe she is,' Janaki said without even looking at me.

'My mother-in-law always said that she should wear long skirts. This dress' – she meant my frock – 'might be all right for Bangalore, she used to say, but it draws attention here, makes her look different from the other girls. You know how it is, we like to think of our girls as children, but outside . . . My mother-in-law was saying exactly that just some days ago, before she fell ill. Will you go and see her sometime, Janaki? She was always so fond of you.'

Janaki only said, 'I think Nithya will wear whatever she wants to,' and turned and went inside. Kodai told me afterwards that Kamala told the others that Janaki, too, was behaving strangely now – 'on edge all the time. But who wouldn't in her place, after all those terrible things happening around her?'

Ambuja Pati's condition, according to reports from Kodai, changed every other day, rising and falling like some whimsical tide. The doctor who tended her had begun to despair that she was unconscious nearly all the time, but then there would be a burst of mysterious energy and she would heave herself forward, sucking and gurgling fiercely at the shore.

Kodai soon tired of it all. I knew this was not really because of her grandmother's illness but because Vasu, who stayed at home because he was less useful at the hospital than his wife, kept a sharp eye on his daughter. Gentle as he usually was, he was beginning to feel obliged to be severe with her. So Kodai found that she had to put a stop to her wanderings in and around the street.

'He doesn't even like me coming to your house

any more, because of all that happened,' she complained to me.

'Then maybe you shouldn't come,' I said.

*　　*　　*

'Janaki wants to see you,' I told Raghu one evening.

She had asked me that morning if I knew how to contact Raghu.

'I need to see him,' was all she had said. I had walked down the street to look for him feeling important, as though I were carrying a crucial secret message.

He knocked at our door at precisely the same time as the last visit. Janaki was more obviously glad to see him this time. Though she didn't say much – Janaki never ever said much, even afterwards – she actually smiled when she saw him. She was beautiful when she smiled, as beautiful, young and hopeful as Sudha had been. And I knew she wouldn't let herself die alone and unhappy in a small sunlit room.

But I think that it was from that time that they both merged in my head and became one – Sudha and Janaki, Janaki and Sudha. They were both important to me and I couldn't take sides with either, and I didn't see any need to. They had blended into something grand and new.

'How are you?' Raghu asked, smiling back at Janaki, raising his face to hers.

'Why don't you come in?' she said.

He refused the coffee Janaki offered but drank a whole glass of water instead. I could see that he was beginning to feel more at home here.

Janaki didn't wait too long before asking her question: 'I wanted to know if it would be possible for you

234

to make arrangements for some money for me. It's quite a large sum.'

Raghu seemed surprised but nodded. 'Of course. How much will you need?'

'It is quite a large sum,' she said again apologetically. 'About 10,000 rupees.' She looked closely at his face as if she wanted to see whether that startled him.

'That is not too difficult,' he smiled. I remembered the large house, the two servants and what I had been told about his inheritance.

'So you will be able to arrange a loan? I've heard you know about these things,' Janaki said. Then she added, 'I have just a little bit of gold as security. It is the only jewellery I kept after my husband died.'

It was the first time I had heard her refer to her husband. And if she had been holding on to anything, it fluttered out through the windows, as unimportant as discarded paper.

Raghu hesitated. 'There is no need to think about loans.' He faltered and looked embarrassed. 'I can give you the money – that is, if you're willing to take it from me.'

'No.' Though she refused him, her voice was gentle. 'Let's place the gold as security. Or let's sell it – that would be even better.'

Raghu didn't press her to accept his money, though he wouldn't agree to sell any of the gold. They agreed that he would return in two days. He left through the back door again, but this time we both walked with him to the edge of the garden. Vasu was outside and I knew he could see us, but he was too hassled by all that was happening in his own household to tell Kamala about it – till much later.

235

Raghu came back in two days and said that he had got the money without having to pawn the gold. He could give it to Janaki the next day. It struck me that it was strange that she had been willing to trust Raghu with her jewellery. Amma would never have done that with someone who was practically a stranger. We made our last trip to the temple. The previous visit seemed a very long time ago. I leaned over the railings and peered at the statue of Andal the poetess-saint. They had made her small and frail, with a tender stalklike body lost beneath the folds of a heavy red sari.

'Do they ever take her out in procession?' I turned to ask Janaki.

'Yes, they do. Once a year.'

So the goddess too got tired of the stickiness of her shrine and the softness of the flowers. I looked at the plump priest and imagined him in the procession, how he'd stop to shift the weight on his shoulders and remove his spectacles to wipe the sweat off his face. I had once seen another goddess in another procession, and her wild hair and flaming tongue now grew indistinguishable from this dreamy little face and frail-limbed body.

This time we stayed longer at the stalls. Janaki bought a wooden doll with a bobbing head, a kaleidoscope and, because the ragged little girl who was selling it begged us, a tiny red plastic monkey that could slide up and down a metal wire that was already beginning to rust.

'But what are you going to do with all these things?' I asked in surprise.

Janaki laughed. 'I don't know,' she admitted. But this

was the first time she'd had money to spend without having to account for where it went. She had brought a fifty-rupee note from one of the five thick bundles Raghu had handed us the day before.

'It seems such a large sum of money,' Janaki had said.

'But it won't last for ever,' I had pointed out.

'I know it won't.' She had been more thoughtful for a moment, then shrugged. And she was now looking at the unpredictable loveliness of the reds and pinks and blues at the bottom of the kaleidoscope.

'Janaki! And Nithya!'

It was Sulochana, resplendent in her jewellery. She looked surprised and even mildly disapproving. Janaki had no right to be here at the temple market looking through a kaleidoscope – not after all that had happened. And at a time when people were feeling sorry for her. She looked at Janaki closely and seemed puzzled. But we got away from her quickly.

'Six rupees,' the auto driver said when we got off at our gate.

*   *   *

Many things happened after that in Kodai's house, each incident stumbling breathlessly on the heels of the last. Kamala was very excited to begin with. She looked over the compound wall one morning. I was picking flowers from her creeper and started guiltily when I saw her large, fair face, like a well-fed wood nymph's, appear through the leaves.

'Where is Janaki? I have news for her,' Kamala beamed.

'She is having her bath.'

237

'Is she?' Kamala probably wondered why Janaki was having her bath at this late hour – it was nearly mid-morning.

'Will you tell her that Kodai has had her first period?'

It was a ridiculous message to give anyone, but I told Janaki anyway.

'It will be your turn soon,' Kamala had added encouragingly just before she'd turned away. I didn't tell Janaki *that*, though it had made me seethe with indignation.

Janaki handed me a ten-rupee note to give Kodai. 'Tell her that I want her to spend it on whatever she feels like.' And I went because I did want to see Kodai. It was important to know whether she looked different.

She was sitting in the corner reserved for her, very pleased with herself. She had on a half-sari and a tight blouse – the kind grown-up women wore. I caught a glimpse of a roll of midriff, as plump and quivery as brown jelly. She was pleased when I gave her Janaki's gift, and tucked it into her waist quickly before her mother came in. I wondered how she could look so smug with all those layers of damp cloth torn from her mother's old underskirts stuck between her legs.

'They would have had a celebration for me, you know,' she said importantly, 'if only my grandmother wasn't in hospital now. But Amma has promised me more new clothes later.'

Sometimes, all these years later, I wonder where Kodai is and whether anything ever happened to change the snooping, infuriating child I had known. The eleven-year-old who knew so much, did whatever she wanted to and hardly ever cared to please.

Her brother, I knew, left Thiruninravur for Madras. He left home one afternoon when Vasu was doing his turn at the hospital. He had actually wept a little and embraced his mother goodbye. Kamala had panicked because he hadn't told his father, because he was carrying so little with him, because he was doing this to them now – when his grandmother was so ill.

Ambuja Pati, who seemed to be getting better and lay awake on her hospital bed with her eyes half open, was not told that her only grandson was leaving home, but she had gathered from Kamala's tears and whispered conversations with Vasu that they were worried about Sridhar.

'Let him do whatever he wants, the scoundrel! He'll come to no good in the end, and then he'll learn.' And she had turned her head towards the wall and shut her eyes.

Kamala had begun to weep loudly at that. 'What are you crying so much for? I'm not dead yet,' Ambuja Pati had snapped.

'My amma is really worried something terrible will happen to Sridhar,' Kodai told me.

'He'll be fine,' I said.

'How do you know that?'

'Because I've been to Madras. It's not as scary as all that.'

'It's all the fault of those Catholic priests at his college,' Narayan Mama had apparently told Vasu and Kamala.

'But they know nothing about it. I met them, didn't I?' Vasu had protested.

'They are lying,' Narayan Mama had insisted angrily. 'I know these people. They never tell the truth if they can help it. They have taken your son away to convert him.'

'I don't think they are lying,' Vasu had said wearily.

Sridhar did write to them days later, and Kamala consoled herself with the thought that at least he wasn't sick or dead. Kodai would have liked to have waited by the gate for her brother's return, but she could no longer stay outside as often as she wanted to. Kamala, too, was beginning to keep track of her movements.

'Come in, Kodai. You can't stand there where everyone can see you,' I heard her calling. 'Not any more.'

* * *

Sundar stayed at home for a couple of days with a mild fever. When he came downstairs after that his cheeks were so hollow that his nose was huge on his face. He looked like an exhausted goblin, I thought, a timid ghost that had flitted into a house he'd never belonged to. Too many things had happened to him all of a sudden – Sudha's death, interrogation by the police, his neighbours' and old friends' hostility and now Janaki. His world needed a frame, a structure he could recognize and rely upon. The old one had fallen apart.

When he came down one morning, Janaki was still in the kitchen. I was outside but came in out of curiosity. I had been waiting for them to talk to each other.

'I want to ask you something,' he said. And though she continued whatever she was doing, she waited.

'I noticed last night that the key to the bank locker is not in my room any more.'

'You mean *my* bank locker.' She wasn't upset.

Sundar didn't say anything and I began to think that was all. But after he washed up and returned, he asked, 'So you took the key?'

'Yes, I needed some of my jewellery.'

'Why?'

'I need money. I thought I would pawn it, but Raghu has made other arrangements for me.'

'Raghu! The . . . ?' Sundar was startled.

'Yes. Raghu.'

'I wish you would tell me what's happening in this house all of a sudden!' He had raised his voice. He was angry now.

'Not all of a sudden. It's been happening for a long time. It's just that there are some things you don't notice.'

'What are you talking about, Janaki?'

And I marvelled at how very stupid he was.

'I'm tired – I've been tired for a very long time,' she said steadily. I remembered that she had said that to me once before, a long time ago.

She went on with whatever she had been doing, stopping only to switch off her transistor, which had been on all along. Sundar hadn't said anything about the transistor, though he couldn't have failed to notice it. I heard the crunch of leaves outside and prayed that Kodai wasn't coming – she shouldn't come now, not at this moment. But when I peered out cautiously I couldn't see her, couldn't see anyone at all. I had imagined it.

'*You* are tired! Is that why you told that girl to kill

herself?' Sundar, too, sounded tired. 'It's your fault she died – you told her to kill herself,' he said. 'You know it's your fault.' So he, too, had overheard that exchange with Sudha. I hadn't even known he'd been at home then.

Janaki didn't look up, but some of the milk she was going to boil spilt from the vessel and fell into the fire with a hiss. She was frightened. Something as fragile as glass, something just starting to be built, was about to fall to the ground with a tinkle and a crunch. Even the hums and chirps and sighs from the garden stopped. I waited for one of them – Sundar or Janaki – to say something.

It was Janaki who spoke next. 'It's absurd to think that what she did was because of what I told her. We don't know why the girl killed herself – none of us know exactly why.'

She waited for him to reply. When he didn't, she continued, 'You didn't help her, either, did you, that night she asked you to help? Things might have turned out differently if *you* had done something then.'

'I was scared and upset by what she told me. I didn't know what I was saying. I meant to help her all along; I wouldn't have abandoned her like that. I was quite fond of her . . . None of you knew that.'

I didn't stop to wonder at the loneliness in his voice. I only despised him more than I had ever before.

'She was a fool to trust you. Both of us have been fools,' Janaki said.

'I don't know what you mean, Janaki. I've always tried to do my best for you – like I promised Amma. I'm sorry if you were not happy, but you know there was nothing more I could have done.'

Janaki smiled a strange twisted smile. 'There is no need to be sorry. But you have to know that things will be different now, not like before – before Sudha came,' she said.

It was all quite finished now. Janaki waited for the milk to boil.

'It's getting late for your office. It's already nearly ten o'clock,' she reminded him gently.

Though she didn't follow him to the door I saw that she listened for the sound of his scooter being started, for the drone and soft rattle as it went down the road. She looked a little sad, I thought.

Someone came up to the back door and pushed it open. It was Kodai for real this time.

'Is anyone at home?' she called, and she came right in without waiting for an answer.

Chapter Twelve

Ambuja Pati was dead. When they brought her home from hospital there was a crowd waiting. Vasu struggled with his end of the stretcher, haggled in whispers with the driver of the van, gave up and went in to mourn his mother.

Janaki and I went to see her together. The house was filled with people. A baby began to cry, everyone turned around disapprovingly to look and his mother hurried out of the room. Vasu sat by his mother's side, stunned into silence.

'She brought him up all on her own – he was all she had,' people told each other solemnly several times that day. Kamala cried in loud unexpected fits and Kodai flitted in and out, dry-eyed and quiet, very aware that people were looking at her new half-sari. I suspected that she didn't really mourn the death of her grandmother. Some people actually remarked on the fact that she didn't weep. Kamala resented their comments: 'She *is* unhappy, poor thing,' she said. 'I wish people would leave her alone.'

But when Kodai was called to do something and couldn't be found, Kamala flew into a panic. 'Where is she? Where could she have gone?' she fluttered wildly around the house, forgetting that her mother-in-law had just died.

When Kodai came in through the back door and they asked her where she had been, she said that she'd only gone to Janaki's garden, and only for five minutes – was there any need for them to fuss? I wondered what she was doing in our house when both Janaki and I were here.

But I wanted to look at Ambuja Pati. She was only the second dead person I had seen. Her sari had slipped onto her shoulders, and because she hadn't been able to get her head shaved ever since she fell ill, her white hair was longer than I had ever seen it. She wouldn't have been too happy about that – or would she? None of us would ever know. We only knew that for her, the demands of orthodoxy had been the only way to fill the hours, days and years – saying the thousand names of Vishnu a hundred thousand times, loving her son with a fierce intensity because he was the fruit of her endurance and sacrifice, feeling the rasp of the razor on her scalp every other morning.

She died peacefully, some people said, slipped into it much more easily than she had slipped into sleep for several decades now. But Kodai said that she had been terrified she was going to die, that death was the one thing Ambuja Pati had always been frightened of. 'She once told me that Yama was sitting at the back door waiting for her,' Kodai whispered to me. 'She even made me go and look out the kitchen window one evening to check. But of course there was no one there.'

245

*   *   *

The day after Ambuja Pati died a telegram came from my parents. Janaki signed for it. The project had been completed sooner than they expected and they would be back on Saturday – a week from today. *Will come to take Nithya Tuesday 15th stop*. The postman brought a letter that same afternoon, dated two weeks before. Amma had written much the same thing. They had air tickets right up to Bangalore this time, and needed just one or two days to unpack and clean the house before Amma took a train to Madras and from there to Thiruninravur to take me back.

There was a note just for me, which I took upstairs to read. They were very excited about coming back and seeing me again. They had missed me a lot, Amma said, and had been especially anxious when that terrible incident happened but it was all over now, wasn't it?

I ran my eyes quickly down the rest of the note and went downstairs. I would be home in a week and this house, this town, its people and their lives would come to a standstill because I was no longer there to watch them. Their expressions would be frozen as if they had been drawn with a stick on flattened clay, their hands raised in gestures that would stay incomplete, like characters in a book.

I wandered into the kitchen and out into the garden looking for Janaki. Every day at this time she watered the rose plant she had brought home some days ago and placed in the shadow of the parapet above the kitchen window. A strand of hair had escaped from her plait and hung loose. She looked up at me and said, pushing the hair off her face, 'You saw what your amma wrote in her letter to us. Does she say anything else to you?'

'No. They, or at least Amma is coming here next week to take me back home.'

'You must be happy,' she said.

I didn't say anything to that and she picked up her bucket and went to tend her plant, bending low over it to make certain that water and mud didn't trickle down the sides of the pot. She was thinking hard about something and didn't remember to bring the bucket back inside after she had finished. She went out that afternoon.

The next day Janaki asked me to get Raghu to come again. When he presented himself the next day she didn't waste any time: she wanted him to get us both train tickets. She would take me back home, she announced. Raghu was as surprised as I was.

'What about my amma?' I asked. 'I thought she was coming for me.'

'I've telegraphed your mother and told her I will bring you instead,' she said. She turned to Raghu. 'I went to the station yesterday. All the seats for the dates I wanted were booked.'

'I'll see what I can do,' he promised. 'I have some friends at Arani junction.'

'What if Amma insists on coming herself? What will we do then?' I asked Janaki after Raghu had left.

'Surely Padma will not object to me coming along with you? She'll just be a little – surprised.' She looked at me and smiled the small smile she sometimes smiled nowadays, reserved only for me.

'Don't you *want* me to come with you?' she asked.

'No, I do want you to.' I flushed because I knew I sounded as though I were lying. But I wasn't.

That night I wondered how I really felt about it. I had been looking forward to riding with Amma on the train half-listening to her chatter, pretending not to be interested in her account of her trip, the things that had happened and not happened to her. And I couldn't imagine Janaki actually living with us in the flat in Bangalore.

'Are you going to stay with us?' I'd already asked her.

'For some time – and then I'll think of something else to do. I still have all that money.'

When I woke up the next morning her plans seemed exciting, filled with unexplored promise. Amma telegraphed back to say that Janaki could bring me back. Raghu came with the tickets two days later.

'When are you coming back?' he asked Janaki anxiously.

'I don't know yet.'

And I watched his face fall.

Just before he left Janaki said, 'Please give me your address. I'll contact you.'

He wrote it out for her. Janaki kept it carefully with the tickets and that seemed to reassure him. I noticed that she didn't give him our address in Bangalore.

When Janaki told Sundar she was leaving, he didn't say anything at first. It was as though he had expected it. I also knew that Sudha's father had sent him a postcard the day before saying that he wanted to come to Thiruninravur once more. He needed to talk to Sundar, he said.

'Are you coming back?' Sundar asked Janaki.

'No,' she said. And that was all either of them said about it.

But Sundar came to the station with us. The stationmaster came out, looked at him and said something to the vendor, the same one who had been there when I first came. Sundar waited till the train left. Raghu was also there, and though they and Sundar must have seen each other they didn't speak. Raghu waved when we began to move, more diminutive than ever in the half-light of the high-ceilinged station.

In his fifth avathara Vishnu manifested himself as a dwarf and conquered the three worlds. He grew to gigantic proportions and encompassed the earth with his first stride, the heavens with his second, then placed his foot on Bali's mighty head.

Though neither of us knew it then, Janaki would celebrate the first anniversary of her departure from Thiruninravur by returning there. She wouldn't stay long, and she and Raghu would leave together.

The train gathered speed and I saw the dusty trees, the wells and the mud roads rush by and felt the world jolt and rumble beneath me.

*   *   *

When I came back to Thiruninravur twelve years later, another road had been built into town, making the journey to Madras faster and easier. There were now three garment factories on the outskirts of town, where once there had been only paddy fields and coconut groves. The railway tracks had been converted to broad-gauge and more trains stopped for a longer while at the station. The streets were more crowded and inter-caste clashes were starting to happen, small in scale but frequent enough to make the district authorities anxious.

GC Street had been tarred but the houses were still there. Kamala, Vasu, Sulochana . . . I hadn't forgotten any of their names. I looked carefully at the faces that hurried past trying to see if I could spot someone I had known. But I couldn't recognize anyone, though most of the old residents must have stayed on. Of course, some of them must have died.

I stopped before Sundar and Janaki's house. The gate had rusted and the small strip of compound in front was overgrown with weeds. Sundar had refused to sell the house though he had left Thiruninravur a long time ago. It strained forward into the street as if it couldn't make up its mind whether to give up and fall to the ground. I knew that if I went in with the keys Janaki had given me just before I came, the rooms would smell musty.

Maybe someone would come up to me and tell me that a girl had died in one of those rooms twelve years ago.

'I knew her,' I would then tell them, and watch them look surprised. 'She and I once watched a solar eclipse together.'

I might even tell them about the other woman I knew who had also lived here, and about how I had visited Sundar two years ago and found that he'd let himself become an old man at fifty.

'Come visit us more often,' I had said, and he had looked puzzled. I wondered if he had been even listening to me.

But no one spoke to me, and I realized that I was getting in people's way by standing there. I walked farther down the road and turned into the lane that ran behind the houses. It wasn't tarred yet, but the tamarind grove and its ghosts had disappeared. I thought I might be able to get into the garden from behind, but a wall had been built around the house where the hibiscus bushes had been and I could only see the trees' topmost branches, growing untidily into each other. Just a few feet below, the back of the wall served as a garbage bin. Ripe gooseberries from the overhanging branches topped the heap of paper and plantain leaves still smeared with stale food. A brown cat with a big face and starved body was picking its way through the pile of waste, delicate as a ballet dancer. When it saw me approaching it leapt lightly out of sight, its skinny tail held high.

THE END

THE MISTRESS OF SPICES

Chitra Banerjee Divakaruni

'A DAZZLING TALE OF MISBEGOTTEN DREAMS AND
DESIRES, HOPES AND EXPECTATIONS, WOVEN WITH
POETRY AND STORYTELLER MAGIC'
Amy Ten

'A MARVELLOUS COMBINATION OF MYTH AND
ROMANCE, SOCIAL CRITIQUE AND POETRY'
San Francisco Chronicle

Tilo, an immigrant from India, runs a spice shop in Oakland,
California. While she supplies the ingredients for curries and
kormas, she also helps her customers to gain a more precious
commodity: whatever they most desire. For Tilo is a Mistress
of Spices, a priestess of the secret magical powers of spices.

Through those who visit and revisit her shop, she catches
glimpses of the life of the local Indian expatriate community.
To each, Tilo dispenses wisdom and the appropriate spice,
for the restoration of signt, the cleansing of evil, the pain of
rejection. But when a lonely American ventures into the
store, a troubled Tilo cannot find the correct spice, for he
arouses in her a forbidden desire – which if she follows will
destroy her magical powers . . .

'DIVAKARUNI'S MAGIC [IS] HER ABILITY TO CRAFT
SUCH A COMPLEX TALE WRITTEN SO EXQUISITELY
WITHOUT OVERWHELMING HER READER'
Los Angeles Times

'FASCINATING STUFF . . . APPEALING FLAVOURED AND
COLOURFUL'
Mail on Sunday

'A SPLENDID NOVEL, BEAUTIFULLY CONCEIVED AND
CRAFTED. THIS BOOK IS SO GOOD THAT I WANT TO
READ EVERYTHING SHE HAS WRITTEN BEFORE AND
EVERYTHING SHE WILL EVER WRITE IN THE FUTURE'
Pat Conroy

0 552 99670 X

BLACK SWAN

KISSING THE VIRGIN'S MOUTH

Donna M. Gershten

'A BEAUTIFULLY WRITTEN, LYRICAL NOVEL. THE KIND
OF BOOK YOU INHALE IN ONE BREATH AND CAN'T
FORGET AFTERWARD'
Barbara Kingsolver

WINNER OF THE BELLWETHER PRIZE FOR FICTION

Kissing the Virgin's Mouth is the fictional memoir of
Guadalupe Magdalena Molina Vásquez – wife, scoundrel,
courtesan and mother. In a world where gender and class
roles are rigid, and religion predominant, Magda refuses to be
a victim. She creates a philosophy of life that she can thrive
in, a religion of cynical optimism, pragmatism, and
determined gratitude. Seemingly invincible yet always
fallible, Magda climbs from wide-eyed childhood to worldly
courtesan lifre, from youth to the early onset of blindness in
middle age.

In the Golden Zone of Teatlán, Sinaloa, Mexico, where
tourists and wealthy Mexicans thrive and where poor
Mexicans come only to work or visit the shrine of the miracle
baby Jesus, Guadalupe performs her daily ritual. In the chair
of her beloved Tía Chucha mortared to the roof of her Golden
Zone home, Magda shaves her long legs, tells her life stories,
and thrusts her fierce prayers of gratitude toward the Sea of
Cortés. She recounts her life strategies – seasoned with an
earthy, hard-earned wisdom – so that she might pass them
along to her half-American daughter, Martina, and to her
young Mexican cousin, Isabel.

This is a novel about love, the power of sex, and the struggles
of women. It is about the secrets of survival. It is about what
a woman can do.

'VIVID, SEXY, GENEROUS AND BOLD'
Andrea Barrett, author of *The Voyage of the Narwhal*

0 552 99978 4

BLACK SWAN

COASTLINERS

Joanne Harris

'SHE IS SO TERRIFIC, SHE CAN WRITE ABOUT
ANYWHERE, ANYTHING, ANYONE'
Daily Telegraph

On the tiny Briton island of Le Devin, life has remained
almost unchanged for over a hundred years. For generations,
two rival communities, the wealthy La Houssinière and the
impoverished village of Les Salants, have fought for control
of the island's only beach.

When Mado, a spirited local girl, returns to Les Salants after
a ten-year absence, the finds her home threatened, both by
the tides and the machinations of a local entrepreneur.
Worse, the community is suffering from an incurable loss of
hope.

Mado is not so easily discouraged. Dogged by prejudice from
the superstitious villagers, she is forced to enlist the help of
Flynn, an attractive drifter. But Mado's attempts to transform
the dying community have unforeseen consequences. As Les
Salants returns slowly to life, so do past tragedies, including
the terrible secret that still haunts Mado's father. And is
Flynn really who he says he is?

'A MUST-READ'
Punch

'A WRITER OF TREMENDOUS CHARM . . . A WINNING
BLEND OF FAIRY-TALE MORALITY AND GRITTY REALISM'
Independent

0 552 99885 0

BLACK SWAN

THE JADU HOUSE
Travels in Anglo-India

Laura Roychowdhury

A cultural and confessional journey into the heart of the
Anglo-Indian community in India.

Even today, the Anglo-Indian and Eurasian community in
India – a mixed-race community that stretches back to the
days of the British Raj – is tainted with outcast status. Laura
Roychowdhury travelled to West Bengal to hear their stories.

Part travelogue, part historical inquiry, part love story, *The
Jadu House* explores the tangled web of passion, hatred and
longing that has bound India and Britain together for over
two hundred years.

0 552 99913 X

BLACK SWAN

A SELECTED LIST OF FINE WRITING
AVAILABLE FROM BLACK SWAN

99313 1	**OF LOVE AND SHADOWS**	*Isabel Allende*	£7.99
99921 0	**THE MERCIFUL WOMEN**	*Federico Andahazi*	£6.99
99734 X	**EMOTIONALLY WEIRD**	*Kate Atkinson*	£6.99
99860 5	**IDIOGLOSSIA**	*Eleanor Bailey*	£6.99
99922 9	**A GOOD HOUSE**	*Bonnie Burnard*	£6.99
99824 9	**THE DANDELION CLOCK**	*Guy Burt*	£6.99
99979 2	**GATES OF EDEN**	*Ethan Coen*	£7.99
99686 6	**BEACH MUSIC**	*Pat Conroy*	£8.99
99670 X	**THE MISTRESS OF SPICES**	*Chitra Banerjee Divakaruni*	£6.99
99836 2	**A HEART OF STONE**	*Renate Dorrestein*	£6.99
99925 3	**THE BOOK OF THE HEATHEN**	*Robert Edric*	£6.99
99935 0	**PEACE LIKE A RIVER**	*Leif Enger*	£6.99
99587 8	**LIKE WATER FOR CHOCOLATE**	*Laura Esquivel*	£6.99
99898 2	**ALL BONES AND LIES**	*Anne Fine*	£6.99
99851 6	**REMEMBERING BLUE**	*Connie May Fowler*	£6.99
99978 4	**KISSING THE VIRGIN'S MOUTH**	*Donna Gershten*	£6.99
99890 7	**DISOBEDIENCE**	*Jane Hamilton*	£6.99
99885 0	**COASTLINERS**	*Joanne Harris*	£6.99
99605 X	**A SON OF THE CIRCUS**	*John Irving*	£7.99
99867 2	**LIKE WATER IN WILD PLACES**	*Pamela Jooste*	£6.99
99738 2	**THE PROPERTY OF RAIN**	*Angela Lambert*	£6.99
99862 1	**A REVOLUTION OF THE SUN**	*Tim Pears*	£6.99
99913 X	**THE JADU HOUSE: Intimate Histories of Anglo-India**	*Laura Roychowdhury*	£7.99
99960 1	**WHAT THE BODY REMEMBERS**	*Shauna Singh-Baldwin*	£7.99
99952 0	**LIFE ISN'T ALL HA HA HEE HEE**	*Meera Syal*	£6.99
99864 8	**A DESERT IN BOHEMIA**	*Jill Paton Walsh*	£6.99
77107 4	**SPELLING MISSISSIPPI**	*Marnie Woodrow*	£6.99